I'm David, by the way

Jorgi

ISBN: 978-0-620-73861-3

This story was inspired by Nádine.

CONTENTS

With great thanks to my entire family for their loving support. And special thanks to my sister.

CHAPTER 1: LITTLE BABY

Mary-Kate woke up early, feeling particularly frustrated and depressed. The situation she found herself in, was taking its toll on her, on her husband, and their marriage. Never in her whole life, in her thirty-nine-years on this planet, did she ever imagine that things would get so desperate.

She didn't know which way to turn, or who to turn to!

Her husband has his own unique way of dealing with things, so there was no talking it through or even shouting so loud, that you'll be heard, not to mention being seen!

She felt somehow relieved when she realised that he already left for work. She had no energy for all that awkwardness and the deafening silences. She finally got out of bed and almost dragged herself to the bathroom. She hoped that a quick shower would somehow fix her spiraling emotions.

It did not, so she opted for a hot cup of coffee next. Lucky for her, this stuff was strong, so strong in fact, that it would lift any mood from sub zero to the thirtieth floor! And it did! So she poured another and flopped down in her favourite chair, her thin fingers interlaced around her favourite red coffee cup.

She looked outside, just gazing through the laced window, taking a quick sip now and then. Everything looked so peaceful, so quiet outside, but inside of her, she felt the storm, her storm, building up again.

It felt like anger now, pure red-hot anger, bubbling up inside her, flaming heat at the back of her pale neck. She closed her tired eyes for a moment, took her last sip of the now cooled black liquid.

When she returned her gaze to the inviting world outside, she saw a young boy pedalling past while whistling a happy tune. Her dark eyes suddenly widened, she lowered her red coffee cup and slowly rose while she considered her wild idea...

She knew that she would still fit in her tights, and she also knew that their dusty crash-helmets were somewhere in the overcrowded, or as she called it 'lived-in', basement.

Closing the door behind her, looking like a real cyclist, she decided to go to the nearest park offering bike trails. The nearest one also turned out to be the biggest.

She felt overwhelmed as she started to pedal slowly through the main gate, looking up at the huge wooden nameplate. She wasn't familiar with this park, so she thought it best to stick to the bumpy dirt trail meandering through the thick brush.

Tall trees made it hard to make out bigger rocks on the trail, but she kept going, because the idea was to ride hard and fast in order to clear her webby head.

Due to shaded patches on the trail, and maybe too much caffeine, Mary-Kate did not see the pointy rock that sent her bike hurtling through the forest air. She got acquainted with mother earth in a very rude and painful way.

At first, she lay very still and kept her brown eyes tightly closed, too afraid to open them.

She opened one, then the other, and made out a man's shape hovering above her. He looked concerned, and then a smile, the widest one she ever saw, broke across his face. He held out his gigantic hand in a very gentle manner.

She looked at him, dazed, but then with a trembling hand, she reached out and almost grabbed his arm.

He pulled her to her feet, very carefully, and all the while, Mary-Kate could feel this stranger's strength, but at the same time, it felt soft, ever so gentle.

"Are you all right?" he uttered his first words, as softly and as gently as his touch. She noticed his worn backpack then for the first time, and wondered what *that* was all about.

"I'm fine, thank you. Thank you for coming to my aid," she answered whilst checking herself for any damage. Phew, no broken bones, Mary-Kate thought, lucky for her, she got off lightly with only minor scrapes and bumps, which was probably going to leave some bruises. What a kind reminder...

"I'm David, by the way," said the stranger as he bent down to get a closer look at her twisted mountain bike.

"I'm Mary-Kate. Thanks again for helping me." She tried looking over his broad shoulders and asked: "What's the damage?"

He looked up and smiled. "You won't be riding any

time soon." He lifted her bike as if it was light as a feather and gave her a quick look up and down, and up again.

"Do you live nearby?"

Mary-Kate took a moment before she answered warily, "Yes, a couple of blocks that way," she pointed in the direction of her neighbourhood.

"Are you able to walk that distance?" David asked with genuine concern in his voice. She took a few steps and felt sore, but not in a way that would prevent her from walking home.

"Yes," she said with confidence and they started walking back to the main entrance, with her limping a bit and him carrying her 'wild' bike.

At first they walked in silence, but then curiosity got the better of her. "Were you like camping there?" she asked slowly, cautiously. He burst out laughing. She looked at him confused, but she liked his laughter though. It sounded so genuine, almost familiar.

"No," he finally answered still smiling. "I'm on my way somewhere, the park just happened to be on my path. Lucky for you, it would seem." Mary-Kate could see a certain vibrancy in his light-brown eyes; they are so full of life and have a certain type of lightness. Unlike her heart which felt so heavy these past few months, maybe even years.

They left the park with its green, calm scenery behind and turned onto a busy street – cars honking and noisy engines revving. A red-faced woman walked past them explaining very loudly why she was late for her dental appointment.

"Are you happy?" David asked unexpectedly, bringing her back to the busy sidewalk.

Mary-Kate took a few seconds before she answered

with a frown, "Yes, no, yes, yes, I am happy."

"That didn't sound very convincing," David remarked and looked at her intently. She avoided his eyes, fearing that he may see the hurt and disappointment lurking in her own brown eyes. She didn't know what to say, and she did not want to talk about her problems, especially not with someone she hardly knew!

"Where are you going?" Mary-Kate asked, hoping to change the subject and deflecting some of the attention back to him.

David stared in front of him for what felt like an eternity, before he answered.

"I don't know yet, but I will know once I get there." Even more confused by this enigmatic man, who calls himself David, Mary-Kate once again decided to change the subject.

She knew that by asking too many questions, you open up a door, and you will end up having to answer too many questions yourself!

They were entering her neighbourhood now, and her time grew less and less for getting to know David. She so wanted to know more, especially since being alone most of the time, so she took a chance.

"Where are you from, David?" she asked delicately.

He looked at her intently and then straight ahead before he answered. "By now it feels like I'm from all over," he said while stroking his bushy beard. A smile was still touching his light-brown eyes. There was something in those eyes that she longed for, but she had forgotten what that something was.

She still wanted to ask him why he was on this journey, but they turned onto her street which seemed unusually quiet, even for that time of day. They stopped in front of her house.

David looked at the ordinary house for a long time, and then finally rested his shiny eyes on the garden.

"What a lovely garden!" he remarked full of emotion. "It feels like I'm going to see a little fairy or a laughing gnome at any moment!"

Mary-Kate was surprised by his emotionally charged voice. She studied his face for a few seconds, before she invited him in. It seemed the right thing to do.

Again, he took her by surprise when he answered almost like a child.

"No, thank you. I still have to be somewhere. Where do you want your bike?" She looked around and pointed towards the garage door. David laid her crooked mountain bike on its side and started towards the tree-lined street.

Mary-Kate hastily asked, "Will I ever see you again?" She felt strangely sad that this man, whom she barely knew, was going to leave any minute now.

He turned around slowly and answered with that same soft, gentle voice as before "Where my journey is taking me, I doubt that, but it was nice meeting you. I hope you find whatever it is that you are looking for, Mary-Kate." She could still feel the sincerity of his words, as she watched the backpack disappear around the bend.

She wanted to yell 'thank you', or 'goodbye', or something, but the words would not come.

Still baffled and overcome with emotion, she gingerly tended to her 'wounds'. She cleaned every scrape and put Band-Aids on where necessary. She changed into comfy slacks and a loose t-shirt.

She won't be needing her tights anymore, so she threw them away – they were torn anyway! She walked more easily to the tiny kitchen and made herself a nice cup of tea.

A hearty sandwich followed next; she didn't realise that she was so ravenous. Finishing her second cup of sweet tea, she took a good look around her, and then decided, enough is enough!

She started in the kitchen, the heart of every home, right? Everything had to be clean and shiny, everything. No more slacking! She moved from room to room like someone on steroids, everything had to be neat and tidy and clean!

She was just about to climb down the stairs, aiming for the 'lived in' basement, when the phone rang.

Mary-Kate hurried down the hall, and answered on the third ring.

"Hello, Mary-Kate speaking,"

"Yes, this is she,"

"I'm fine, thank you. And you Doctor?"

"The results, oh yes, Doctor Brown, my results,"

"Oh, really. Are you sure Doctor?"

"Oh, well then, thank you Doctor Brown. Thank you for your call"

"Okay, thank you. You too. Bye."

She hung up the receiver in slow motion, and walked to the nearest chair in slow motion, and sat down in slow motion. She remained motionless for a good while, her whole face twisted in disbelief and total shock.

Then the tears came, slowly at first.

But then all hell broke loose, and Mary-Kate cried like she never cried before. It was raw emotion that swept through her whole body. She started shaking uncontrollably, and the sobs grew even more intense, until finally they stopped.

A cautious smile started pulling at one corner of her mouth. Then she heard the familiar click of the front door and looked up...

Mary-Kate's husband walked through the red front door, and placed his keys in the little glass bowl by the door. He was about to hang up his coat, when he saw his wife.

He was taken aback by what he saw. Mary-Kate sat with her arms around her legs, Band-Aids sticking out, some scrapes here and there. Her dark eyes were all puffy and red.

But what got him the most wasn't her tear streaked face, but the odd expression on her face.

He couldn't make sense of this strange emotion, so he stepped closer slowly, unsure of what to expect.

"Oh, John," Mary-Kate jumped up from the wooden chair and threw her arms around his neck. "I missed you," she whispered in his ear.

He dropped his coat and his leather briefcase on the shiny floor. She pulled him into the living room and said in a very upbeat voice, "Come, come sit with me." They sat down opposite each other and John looked at her cautiously, but also curiously.

"Mary-Kate, what happened to you?" he asked, his voice thick with concern.

"Oh, this, just a little accident, nothing serious. How was your day?" she asked genuinely interested.

He was still baffled by this sudden change in his wife's behaviour. What happened, what came over her, John wondered.

"It was very busy at work today. You know that contract I told you about?" She nodded almost impatiently, but he continued unhindered by this – he just felt so glad to be talking and talking about something else other than 'the topic'!

"The client, a very important..."

"John," Mary-Kate could not wait any longer. "John, I have something to tell you." His face turned back into caution again, his eyes narrowed as he focused on her lips. "Doctor Brown phoned earlier today with my test results."

She paused for a moment, gathering her strength for what may or may not come. "The tests were all positive. I'm pregnant!" and with uncertain enthusiasm, she added, "we're going to have a baby!"

At first, there was no reaction as John's brain took a few seconds to process this important news.

As soon as the shock wore off, great relief washed over him like a wave from the ocean. Becoming more nervous over his delayed reaction, Mary-Kate stood up and searched his face for any sign of emotion.

She gave a huge sigh of relief when she saw the smile appearing on his clean-shaven face.

Finally, overcome with emotion, he almost stumbled into her waiting arms. They hugged each other like it was the end of the world. "I love you, Mary-Kate Sidopolous," he breathed into her ear.

"I love you too," Mary-Kate answered, pressing herself into his arms even harder, kissing his neck softly...

Waking up that morning, she would never have guessed that this day would end so gloriously – her feeling human again, having her best friend and lover back, AND her becoming a mother!

CHAPTER 2: MOVIN' ON UP

It was still dark when John left for work. He would tell himself that it was not his decision, that his wife drove him out. But it was in fact his decision. He could not bear yet another morning with that long face, and those dark resentful eyes.

So he chose to escape to a little street vendor who sold coffee near the harbour. He was obviously way too early for the ferry, so he stood waiting at the guardrail, drinking his piping-hot coffee.

His long coat flapped in the wind. His eyes wandered across the vast ocean and he could hear how the gentle waves lapped against the rocks beneath. That was just what he needed – some alone time to get his head clear, not only for the busy day ahead, but also for his own peace of mind.

He became aware of the increasing activity all around him, and it brought him back to earth. John saw a number of cars waiting to get on the ferry that was now inbound. Everybody stepped closer, even John, with his head feeling crystal clear.

He aimed for his favourite spot, but before he could take his seat, a young boy bumped into him. The youngster was running and therefore not paying attention. John dropped his thick newspaper, and tried to get to it amidst all the busy feet.

Suddenly, a big hand reached out, holding his newspaper. He looked up into a bearded smile and a worn backpack sticking out.

"Thank you," John said while taking back his slightly smeared newspaper. He still wanted to scold the rude youngster, but the boy just ran off. Reading his newspaper every morning before work, was so routine for him and it was one of his highlights.

He felt mildly irritated. He did not want to loose his clarity nor his calm. The stranger held out his hand for a second time and introduced himself.

"I'm David, by the way. And you're welcome." John looked at him surprised and shook his hand. What a grip!

"I'm John. I don't remember seeing you here before," he said while claiming his favourite seat on the ferry.

David sat down beside him, looking at the busy people getting seated, while some chose to stand outside at the guardrail; they probably liked the fresh ocean air, he thought, or is it the ocean itself?

John looked over at him (the stranger), waiting for an answer. It would seem that he was either lost in thought or downright rude! Either way, John had his newspaper waiting for him, filled with the latest news, or should he say 'doom and gloom' - there's a lot of that going around these days. Even at home. Let's not go there, he told himself and picked up his newspaper. Hopefully it would take his mind off things. He really needed a clear head today. He was determined to close that deal!

Somewhere between pages three and four, he heard the most unexpected question of all time.

"What do you want?" David asked.

Those four simple words sent him on an internal journey that he did not want to take! Now it was his turn to answer a question with silence.

At first, John wanted to get offended by this stranger's uncalled for question. But then he realised that it was a fair question to ask, and if he was honest with himself, or even willing to look at the truth staring right at him, right then, he would answer that fearful question.

All of a sudden, he felt greatly annoyed by that stupid question, and by the man who dared ask it!

There goes his calm and his clear-headedness!

He gave David what he thought to be a dirty look, but what he saw, made him feel childish and lame instead.

The man looked at him with so much sincerity and warmth, maybe kindness, he had to look away. That was not what he expected. He was not prepared for that!

He considered saying something, for an instant, but then opted to bury himself in his worldly newspaper.

He tried, as hard as he could, but he could not forget those four little words, and their implications. He knew full well that there would be major consequences for him, his wife, and their marriage if he answered that hard question.

"It was nice meeting you, John. I hope things will become clear for you, so you may find contentment."

Those were David's last words to John, and they left a deep impression on him.

He could still hear the genuineness of his words when he entered his disorderly office.

Anyone could see that John had been working very hard on his latest deal. He thought that he would prepare some more for the upcoming meeting – these were very big 'would be' clients.

As he worked, he began to realise that his mind felt especially sharp right then, even his nerves felt calm, relaxed. He also felt unusually confident, which was new to him.

Wow, he thought, what a welcome change.

He really liked it and secretly hoped that it would last. This could be very beneficial for the meeting - which was scheduled for ten that morning - and it could give him the outcome he desired!

The important meeting took longer than he anticipated, but John ploughed right through.

There was a lot of pulling this way, and a lot of pulling that way. Some hard words fell. Promises were made; some terms were altered or even completely scrapped.

But in the end, after all was said and done, everybody left the table smiling, most of all the new client! John felt relieved, like a heavy burden had been lifted. He also felt extremely proud of himself for keeping his cool, and most importantly, for closing the deal!

He decided to take a late lunch, a little celebratory lunch, just for him. Besides, he felt ravenous as a wolf! It must be all the adrenaline pumping through his veins. Using so much energy, takes its toll on a man, especially this man.

And there he goes again... thinking about his wife, their marriage, 'the topic'.

That's what it was now, a topic. He immediately closed that door SHUT. He did not want to ruin his great lunch, and maybe, just maybe, he could bathe in the glow of his recent success a little while longer.

Back at the office, John decided to return phone calls and check his emails. Luckily, nothing urgent, so he could take his time. Next he tackled his untidy desk, in order to create some space for new documents he knew were coming.

He was busy moving a pile of boxes filled with documents, when he heard a tap on his open door. He turned around and saw his boss standing in the doorway.

"Oh, hi. Come in, Phil. Let me just move these files so you can sit down." Phil waited patiently, but then he 'let fly' and congratulated John on a job well done.

"The bigwigs are very pleased with you for landing that major contract. You know, Leyland & Leyland, aren't just any clients. They are THE CLIENTS. You are now in the pound seats, and that is why you are getting the promotion you've been waiting for. Congratulations, John!"

They shook hands and John could not help but smile from ear to ear. Not only did he land the client of the year, but being promoted for it!

Wow!

He thanked his boss, and he could feel his heart racing. It was beating so fast, he thought it would jump out of his chest from all the day's excitement.

"Why don't you leave early and go celebrate. You deserve it," his boss encouraged him.

"Thank you, Phil. I'll think about it," John answered

back, but knowing John, he would probably not even consider it and stay until late, as usual.

"Do more than just think about it, John, do it!" Phil insisted and left.

Once again, he had a lot to think about, but being John, he just resumed his daily duties and soon forgot about these plaguing thoughts.

Halfway through a lengthy balance sheet, he saw his morning paper sticking out from beneath a blue ledger. The whole ferry-episode came rushing back to him, the rude youngster, David (the unusual stranger), and that nagging, nagging question!

John finally decided to ask the damn question, AND answer it. Why not? It couldn't hurt to, could it?

'What do I want?' he asked himself.

To his surprise, it was not that difficult to answer, and interestingly enough, he already knew the answer. He just did not want to look at it, at that sticky truth.

Being guided by his answer, John grabbed his coat and his leather briefcase, and left his office. The streets were not crammed with people and cars, not yet anyway. So, John hurried to catch the next ferry home.

Home. It sounded so strange then.

Home. It felt more like a boarding house, and nothing else, nothing more, he realised and that shook him deeply. It wasn't supposed to be like this. Mary-Kate was supposed to be the love of his life, his best friend, the woman he shared all of his dreams with.

What happened? What went wrong? He remembered how it all started, but how did it get so messed up, so quickly?

He boarded the ferry, which was fairly quiet, with only a few cars itching to get home.

Was he itching to get home, he asked himself. In his

heart, that happened to be the case. He dearly wanted to embrace his wife like a husband should. Tell her about his exciting day. His successful deal. His long awaited promotion.

He wanted to tell her how much he loved her, and assure her that everything would be all right, for both of them. He wanted to tell her to screw 'the topic', and just be themselves again.

Let whatever happens, happen.

Who knows, maybe this time it will work, because it comes from the heart, and not from some insane, distorted longing. A longing that has consumed his wife to such an extent, that he found it increasingly difficult to recognise her. Not even mentioning, to communicate with her.

He stood up from his favourite seat and joined the others at the popular guardrail. He breathed in the fresh ocean air, hoping that it would clear his head too. He felt the mist rising from the water being disturbed by the giant propeller. This calmed him a bit.

His eyes searched the outstretched body of water, trying to figure out where it stopped and the sky began. The sun was loosing some of its brightness as it started its downward path towards the earth.

John still felt uneasy when they neared the shore. The prospect of going home to his wife was not the only thing that kept him off-balance. His newfound freedom, which felt so unusual to him, also kept him off-balance.

But he decided that he would take one step at a time, figuratively as well as literally speaking. He felt glad that the walk home would take him about fifteen minutes, and if he walked even slower, it could take him twenty, easily.

He shook his head and could not help but smile at his own cowardice.

Turning onto his well known street, he paused again. Weighing his options one by one, and weighing them again just to be sure. He remembered what David had asked him earlier that day.

"What do I want?" he asked himself softly.

I WANT MY LIFE TO BE GOOD AGAIN! What a revelation! What a relief! How long has it been since he had that – a good life? Months? Years? Years it would seem, many years!

He realised that David having asked that question was justified, after all. And not a moment too soon, because for now, he finally had clarity.

A clear vision of what he wanted. He also felt that by getting what he wanted, he would find contentment. Quite possibly for the rest of his life.

He came to a stop five paces from his own front door. He looked at the house. It wasn't the biggest one around, but it was at least decent.

He looked at the exquisite garden and could not help but see Mary-Kate's hand in it. John couldn't understand why that beauty existed only in their garden and not also in his wife. Or even in their marriage.

He once again remembered David's stirring question, and having answered it, honestly, he decided to tell his wife about his exciting day, and hopefully it would lift her spirits, even for a little while.

He also hoped that it would lead to other confessions, like 'I love you'; like 'I want you back in my life'.

If only he could remain strong long enough to do so.

Before his small mind could whisper some nonsense

in his ear, he took those last few brave steps to the red front door...

CHAPTER 3: MEET ME HALF-WAY

Rose tried calling her daughter for the third time that day. Voicemail. Ugh. She hated this voicemail-business. It's just an excuse not to talk to someone.

Whatever happened to the good old days when things were so simple? You phoned someone, they picked up and you had your conversation. So simple, yet so satisfying.

She'll try again after their daily walk, she thought. She looked at her delicate wristwatch.

"Just look at the time," she said to herself, surprised. "It's time for lunch. I hope Betsy is on her way; I don't want to be late."

Just then, she heard a light knock on her door, and Betsy walked in.

"Just in time," Rose greeted her.

"Hello Rose. I had to wait for my prescription to be filled. I hope you didn't have to wait too long. Let's go, dear, I feel a bit faint."

"Oh, Betsy," Rose responded and they walked together, arm-in-arm, to the smart dining room.

They sat at their usual table, hands folded and resting on the floral tablecloth, waiting for their food to be dished up. They looked with great anticipation when it was their turn, but felt disappointed when they saw their plates.

"Oh, dear God," Rose cried out. "You would think that farmers didn't grow vegetables anymore!" Betsy laughed at her friend's pretended tirade. "I mean, I know you're supposed to be grateful and all that, but whatever do you call this mushy business?"

"I don't know, Rose, but I'm sure that it won't be a bother to our dentures, at least." They both started laughing and Rose felt glad that she had a friend like Betsy. Someone who understood her, and who put up with her arduous nature.

Even though they felt that they could eat, they each ate only a small amount. After they finished their 'delicious' lunch, they decided to rest for a bit. So they each went to their own rooms and closed their doors.

Rose only pretended to go take a nap. She felt that only babies needed to nap, not Rose Blumenthal. Besides, she enjoyed the quiet. It gave her time to think.

These days, she had a lot of time on her hands and Lord knows, she had a lot to think about! Being her age, there was no shortage of memories. And lucky for her - sometimes not so lucky - she was able to remember everything.

Lately though, Rachel, her daughter, was on her mind a lot. Rachel, my dear Rachel, she thought and tried to imagine her face in front of her. She almost reached out to touch it.

Why was it so hard to reach her, to break down those years and years of heartache and the never-ending resentment?

Rose suddenly felt tired, so tired. She really felt her seventy years, which said a lot, because normally she wouldn't associate herself with her age.

Imagine that, seventy years old. In her heart she still felt like a young girl. Like the young girl she once was, before her life was turned upside down, before she became so hard...

Betsy always told her, "Rose, don't be so prickly". Oh, Betsy, Rose sighed, she was a true friend. She felt so lucky, considering that to have friends, or even one friend, these days were a luxury!

She saw that it was almost time for their daily walk. Rose wondered whether Betsy was up yet. She switched to her comfortable walking shoes and checked herself in the mirror, before she locked her bedroom door. She was a very private person, therefore she didn't trust easily.

Betsy was indeed up, sitting in her easy-chair tying her shoelaces.

"Did you have a good nap, Betsy?" Rose asked attentively.

"Yes, thank you dear," she stood up and stuffed a pink handkerchief in her pocket. She closed the door behind them and they walked cheerfully through the colourful corridors towards the main gate.

Finally outside the retirement home, Rose felt that she could breathe more easily and she immediately took a couple of deep breaths.

They started walking briskly while they chatted light heartedly. This was, next to a visit from a loved one, probably the highlight of their day, which they both enjoyed tremendously!

They walked their usual route and at that time of

day, it was usually not so busy. Rose loved this neighbourhood with its tree-lined streets and all the houses that appeared so well looked after, each with their own neat garden. She and Betsy would usually stop to admire the beautiful gardens and they would even smell the fragrant flowers.

She missed those days of running her fingers through the soft soil and planting little flowering plants; to nurture them and watch them grow, almost like children...

"My son phoned," she heard Betsy's voice and immediately paid attention. She knew how important Paul was to Betsy.

"They are going on holiday to a friend's cabin up at Lake Bell. Do you know it, Rose?" Betsy asked while they came to a sudden stop.

Rose was fiddling in her little pink moon bag and retrieved a single banknote. Betsy looked curiously at the whole affair – her friend Rose Blumenthal, was going to give money to a beggar standing at the corner of the rather quiet intersection.

Her hand touched his when she gave him the single note.

"Thank you, Miss Rose, but you need this more than I do," the beggar said while placing the note in her hand and gently folding her wrinkled fingers over it. Rose looked surprised, that was not the reaction she expected, but before she could respond, he continued.

"I don't want your money, Miss Rose. I'm standing here, waiting for that traffic light to turn green," he said smiling with so much sincerity in his voice. Rose looked even more surprised, but she also felt silly for thinking that he was just someone looking for a handout.

"How do you know my name?" she asked, trying to mask her silly feelings and for making a blunder. She, Rose Blumenthal, did not make blunders like that!

"I heard your lovely friend call you Rose, Miss Rose. I'm David, by the way," the stranger said in a caring voice.

"I'm Betsy," Betsy interrupted quickly. "Now we all know each other." She looked David over and asked curiously "Why the backpack? Are you some sort of hiker?" He laughed.

"No, maybe in a sense. I'm on my way somewhere, and I like to be prepared," he said with a little twinkle in his light-brown eyes.

"Why do you say that I need it more?" Rose asked sternly.

"Because you have more time left on your clock than you know," David answered politely.

Rose looked at him even more baffled and asked in a harsh tone, "How would you know how much time I have left? What do you know about me, Mr. David what's-your-name?"

David took a deep breath and almost sighed his words, "Put your thorns away, Miss Rose, they are not needed here." Rose was stunned with complete silence.

She looked at David precariously, her light blue eyes narrowed and her thin lips tautened. Betsy cringed inwardly, she knew her friend, so she knew very well what was coming next.

How wrong she was!

Betsy saw tears welling up in those striking blue eyes. At first Rose wanted to explode and tell this stranger 'his fortune', but then something came over her, something surreal happened to her.

David's words finally sank in, and her thick walls

started to give way; give way to something. She didn't know what, yet. She felt Betsy's warm arm around her shoulders, and her tears flowed freely then.

What is happening to me, she thought, and tried her best to get a grip on herself.

David stepped closer and whispered in her ear, "Just let it go, Miss Rose, just let it go." She looked at him with great concern, in her heart she knew his words to be true, but her mind refused to let go.

He touched her hand, lightly, and gave it a gentle squeeze. She relaxed completely and felt like a heavy burden had been lifted from her chest, from her life really!

Rose Blumenthal, could feel her heart again for the first time in many, many years! She could see clearly what she has become, and how desperately she wanted to be that young girl again, before the thorny walls came up.

She realised that she felt light inside, light as a feather. Her heart felt like it was smiling, like it was beaming. She felt for an instant like that young, vibrant girl, she remembered so clearly now.

Rachel, oh my God, Rachel, she suddenly remembered. She felt an overwhelming love for her daughter, like she never felt before *and* an unusual urge to talk to her – today still!

"Rose, dear, are you all right?" she heard Betsy's voice and it sounded so beautiful, so full of warmth. She turned towards Betsy and gave her a smile that reached all the way to her moist eyes.

"Oh Betsy, my dear Betsy. You are my best friend and I am so grateful for that. Thank you," she said and gave Betsy a firm hug. When she turned around to thank David, the dark haired stranger was nowhere to be found. He left without them noticing, backpack and all!

They still looked around for him, but finally convinced, they returned home.

They got back to the retirement home later than usual and decided to quickly visit the ladies' room first of all, to freshen up before dinner. Rose entered her room and it was like she saw it for the first time.

It was tiny and therefore crowded with all her earthly belongings. She even had a wall dedicated to all her books. She loved to read, hence the rows and rows of books. She opened a window to let the cool breeze fill her room with all the lovely fragrances carried from the well-kept gardens.

Tomorrow, Rose thought, I'm going to rid this room of unwanted and unnecessary things. Things other people can use and maybe even enjoy. This excited her and she looked forward to doing just that. She still wanted to phone her daughter; the urge to talk was still there, but first, dinner, it was time for dinner and she did feel rather famished.

She joined Betsy at their usual table and didn't even care what food they got. She was grateful that she could spend meal-time with her best friend!

They talked about their families and their wellbeing. They even talked about Rose spring-cleaning her room, but the largest part of their conversation was about David, the unusual stranger. This man, whom she hardly knew, came out of nowhere and changed her life in an instant!

"I would have liked to thank him, Betsy, but I suppose I won't get that chance," Rose told her dear friend.

"Yes, Rose, it would seem so. But I feel that there's a reason for that, and I suspect that David knows that you're thankful. He doesn't seem the type who needs to be buttered." This eased Rose's conscience a bit. They resumed their pleasant conversation over a tasty bowl of vegetable soup, complete with soft white bread rolls!

After their hearty supper, Rose and Betsy sat down with the other elderly residents, to watch the news, and as always, the weather. They usually watched one or two more programs following the news, but Rose excused herself – she had an important phone call to make.

Betsy winked as she said goodnight, as if to say 'good luck'. Rose returned her goodnight with a brave smile. She walked to her empty room and closed the door behind her. For what came next, she would need privacy and time to set things right with her daughter.

But more than that, time and privacy, she needed courage to say the right words and the determination to resolve this unfortunate situation once and for all. The only way she could do that was by facing the cause of all this unhappiness and resentment.

For years she dreaded facing that unspeakable truth, but she dreaded the phone call where she had to address the 'horrible lie', even more. But after the David-incident, Rose felt differently.

She wasn't afraid anymore and she desperately wanted to set things right between them, before she clocked out! She also felt, strangely enough, that whatever the outcome, whatever the reactions, whatever the words, she, Rose Blumenthal, would have peace.

She would finally have peace.

She picked up the grey receiver; she felt tiny butterflies in her belly, but pressed on and dialled her daughter's phone number for the fourth time that day.

"Hello, Mother," she heard Rachel's voice and her heart skipped a beat...

CHAPTER 4: A MOTHER'S LOVE

Rachel headed out for a quick smoke break. Today was going to be a long day, one of *those* days, she thought! These past few weeks were very stressful for her. She had to work overtime a lot of those days.

Ever since Dean died, she had to do her utmost best to keep this boat afloat. Sometimes it felt like she was thrown into the deep end, and she must admit, having a man around sure made life a hell of a lot easier!

Rachel knew that she shouldn't say such things, but she just missed him *so* much! And what about poor Lily, her sweet Lily. She hardly had any time for her child. She felt so bad and so guilty about that.

What could she do? It seemed so unfair, so unfair to both of them. It would seem that life was unfair.

It started very early for her, losing her father at such a young age, 'the horrible lie' that followed which also drove a wedge between her and her mother. Then there was Dean's passing, which was very hard on her and Lily. She felt blessed having Lily in her life, especially now. She could not bear being alone, not after her husband's sudden death, and her sweet Lily was truly such a good kid!

She looked around while she finished her cigarette. It was your typical day here in the city. The streets were busy with noisy cars coming and going. People were weaving on the sidewalk like busy little ants. Tall, dull buildings completed the picture, except for the golden rays of the mighty sun which enveloped some parts of the otherwise grey surroundings.

Rachel spotted a bearded man with a worn backpack coming her way. Normally she wouldn't pay any attention to the people passing her by, seeing that her head was always so busy, but this man stood out. She couldn't quite explain it, but for some reason he drew her attention... Maybe it was his backpack, but she couldn't be sure.

"Do you have another?" he asked after he came to a standstill in front of her while gesturing with his head towards her cigarette. Rachel looked at him a bit surprised; he did not strike her as the type. She took one out for him and one more for herself; she decided to have another – why not?

She held out the thin Camel and got her lighter ready. When the stranger took it from her, their hands touched briefly. She lit her own cigarette, while he cupped his hands around hers.

"Thank you," she said in an impersonal manner. She gave him the plastic lighter, but he just waved his hand and stuffed the cigarette in his pocket.

"No, thank you," he said softly. "I'll save it for later, for a rainy day." He laughed and leaned against the brick wall next to her.

Rachel looked at him and frowned. "You're a strange

man."

"I know, I have been told so many a time," he said smiling. His sincere smile was reflected in his light-brown eyes. This was rare, Rachel thought. She frowned even more.

"You shouldn't frown like that," the stranger said interrupting her thoughts. "It spoils your lovely face."

She stared at him surprised, taken aback by his sincere words. Normally she would get upset by unwanted attention, but this man was obviously not flirting. What did he want, she asked herself. Did he want money? She couldn't help him there, because one lousy income was all she had, and that was barely enough for the two of them.

The wind suddenly picked up and a loose curl landed on her freckled cheek. For some reason, the dark haired stranger wanted to tuck the unruly curl behind her ear. He stopped himself, and just appreciated her shiny copper hair instead.

Why did he feel this way? He knew he was on an important journey and that to have commitments wasn't a part of the deal.

"I'm David, by the way," he said in an attempt to stop these feelings which were accompanied by the same thoughts.

"I'm Rachel, Rachel Morris. Pleased to meet you," she said and held out her hand. David was reluctant, almost scared to take her hand, but he did so in the end, just to prove to himself that he could rise above his feelings.

"Why do you smoke?" he asked, thinking it better to talk about her.

She kept silent for a bit, then turned towards him and said in a capitulating manner, "It wasn't always the case, me smoking. I started after my husband's death." David saw a certain vulnerability in her beautiful eyes. They reminded him of a forest, so immensely green and full of life!

"I'm sorry for your loss," he said with a comforting expression on his bearded face.

"Thank you," she said, again with the same vulnerability. For some reason, she felt that she could trust 'Back-packer David', and bare all. So, that's exactly what she did.

She told him everything, about her lying mother whom she despised, about her one true love, Dean, who was taken so abruptly. She felt like she was still reeling from his death. About her sweet Lily, who made all of her hardships worthwhile.

"Wow, all that from one simple question. It seems that it was an important question to ask, after all. You have a lot to carry around, don't you? Your backpack is just invisible to the naked eye." Rachel laughed and it felt good, so good. She had forgotten what that was like.

She felt even more intrigued by this strange man, who made her feel at ease, so completely at ease. He made her feel as though time did not exist, as though her troubles did not exist, but that she, Rachel, did exist in every sense of the word, and it felt GREAT!

"Is it not time for you to lighten your overfilled backpack, and get rid of some of that excess weight? Is it not time for you to live again? Rachel, you deserve to," David expressed his words strongly and as ever, sincerely. She suddenly remembered the time.

"Oh my God, David, I have to get back to work. Sorry, I would have loved to continue this conversation, but I must leave right now. Do you have a number where I can reach you, or perhaps an address?" she asked feverishly, her green eyes dancing all over the place.

"Maybe we will meet again, maybe not, but for now, go and find your happiness again. Live again, Rachel. You have your daughter to think about." She had to go, and therefore she had no choice, but to accept these last words from him.

And so, she reluctantly said goodbye to 'Back-packer David', and left. David stood there silently for a few more moments – he will surely remember green-eyed Rachel Morris with her beautiful red curly hair – and then headed for the nearest bus stop.

Rachel was completely wrong about her day, it turned out to be quite all right. Her work load was decent for the day. She even got a smile from her otherwise grumpy boss when he told her that she could knock off early for the day. She was very pleased about going home early, because it would give her a chance to spend more time with Lily.

When she got home, Lily was busy doing her homework. She had more homework than the previous year, and it kept her busy, especially studying for tests. She wanted good grades, because Rachel told her that if she did get them, she could go to college.

"Hi, Mom," Lily greeted her mother. "I thought I heard the garage door. You're home early." Rachel smiled and greeted Lily, she felt genuinely happy to see her daughter.

"How was your day, sweetheart?" she asked while

placing her handbag and keys on the kitchen counter.

"It was good," Lily answered. "But tell me why you're so early," she asked with a frown.

"Why don't you make us some coffee while I go and change, then I will tell you all about it," Rachel proposed and left to go change into something more comfortable.

Lily switched the machine on and made coffee for them. It was something she loved to do, especially when she had to study for an important test. She poured the coffee when she saw her mother taking a seat in their cosy lounge. She carried the plastic tray and placed it gently on the only table in the centre of the room.

Rachel helped herself, and got comfortable on the two-seater sofa. She took a slow, satisfying sip from her huge coffee mug – this child knew how to make good coffee! Lily felt pleased seeing her mother's contentment.

"You won't believe the day I've had." Her mother's voice finally broke the silence. "My grumpy boss, bless his soul, told me that I could leave early, because of all the overtime. So I did. I thought that it would be nice to spend some time with you. We can get some pizzas for dinner, if you want," she said hesitantly, because she knew that it was a weeknight and Lily had a lot of homework.

"Strangely enough, we didn't get a lot of homework, and my studying is up to date. So, I think it's a wonderful idea! I love pizza, I mean, who doesn't?" Lily said with her blue eyes shining even brighter.

"Did something else happen?" she asked. She could see that her mother was somehow different, good-different. Rachel's green eyes lit up when she told Lily about David, and about their unusual conversation. She also told Lily about the impact it had on her, and in fact, still has.

"What happened to him?" Lily asked curiously, she wondered where this was going.

"I don't know," Rachel replied perplexed. "I had to return to work, and that was the last I saw of him. I don't know if I'll ever see him again. 'Backpacker David'," she mused while shaking her head slowly and her green eyes looked off into the distance.

"Mom, Mom," Lily's young voice brought her wandering attention back. "When are we going to get the pizza?" Rachel looked at her watch and had a bizarre thought.

"Why don't we get pizzas on our way to Grandma and surprise her?"

Okay, now I'm officially concerned, Lily thought. What happened to her mother? Why was she acting so strangely?

"I think it's okay," she said slowly, uncertain whether it was really okay.

She knew the tensions that existed between them; she really had no desire for any arguments. She desperately wished that they would just address and fix the problem, and move on. Life was too short for such nonsense. It can be taken in an instant – she thought of her dad, and how much she missed him. He would know what to do!

Half an hour later, the two of them were in her little yellow car, which was getting on in years, on their way to their favourite pizza place.

At Tony's they ordered their usual: two large

vegetarian pizzas with extra mushrooms, plus one for Grandma. Hopefully she would like it. According to Rachel and Lily, these were simply the best pizzas in town. Rachel also got some soda which would compliment the pizzas nicely.

Ten minutes later they stopped in front of the elegant retirement home with its lovely old trees. Rachel had just parked her little car, when her cell phone rang. She was surprised to see the number, but answered anyway.

"Hello, Mother," she said civilly, and thought to herself, what a strange coincidence!

"Hello, Rachel. How are you?" Rose asked hesitantly, not sure what to expect.

"I'm fine. Listen, Lily and I are actually outside, and on our way in..."

"What? You're here. Now?" Rose asked surprised, and wondered about the reason for their visit.

"Yes, Mother. We'll see you inside," and she hung up. They were in a hurry to get to Grandma's room – no one likes cold pizza!

Rose waited in the main hall, and when she saw the pizza boxes, she directed them to the empty dining room.

"Hello, Rachel. Hello, Lily. What an unexpected surprise!" Rose was genuinely happy to see them, and she gave each a hug – Lily's hug was more meaningful.

"Hi, Gran," she said. "How are you? We brought pizza, I hope Gran can manage a whole pizza," Lily said laughingly.

"I'll do my best, Lily Anne. Let me organise some plates and glasses, and then we can talk," Rose answered and disappeared into the large industrial-like kitchen. A few minutes later, she came through the swing doors with white plates, knives and forks, as well as a few glasses.

They ate their pizzas with great enthusiasm, while they talked about school and work, keeping it light. Rose talked about her best friend, Betsy, and all their activities at the retirement home.

After dinner, Rachel suggested to Lily that she go and play the piano for the few residents still in the large lounge area, she did that sometimes and they really loved it!

The moment Lily left, Rachel started to speak, softly at first. "Mother, we need to talk."

"I know, I wanted to all day, so it is very fortuitous that you decided to come and visit me, tonight of all nights. The strangest thing happened today and since then I felt this urgent need to set things right."

Rachel listened intently, she didn't know this side of her mother. She was glad that her mother went first, and she was curious to hear what she had to say. She could also sense that something was different about her mother.

"You know that horrible lie I told you? You never..." Rose was cut short by her daughter, Rachel.

"How can I forget? It's probably the worst lie a parent can tell a child, and you did that to me, YOU!" Rachel spoke louder now and her freckled cheeks looked flushed.

Those last words stung, and Rose looked down. She thought that she could face the ugly truth, but it was harder than she anticipated.

"How could you lie about something like that? There is no justification for that, none! Telling a little girl that her father was dead, just to find out many years later, that he was alive and well, all along!

Mother?!" Rachel suddenly realised that her voice was being carried into the corridor.

Rose's blue eyes started to fill with agonising tears. Hearing her harsh, but honest words tore at her very soul and it made her feel helpless. What could she possibly say to make this right, what words on earth could heal her dear child's heart?

"When I met your father, I thought that I had met my soul mate. For the first time in my life, I felt complete and totally loved by this man. So I gave him my all, all my love, all my trust and all of my dreams." Rose was surprised when she heard her own words, they sounded so sincere, they almost overwhelmed her.

But she kept going – she knew it was now or never.

"So when he packed his suitcase and walked out the door, never to return, it felt like my whole world was collapsing all around me, and there was nothing I could do! For a long time I felt that I was the cause; that there was something wrong with me; that I didn't love him enough. Then one day, when I finally realised that he wasn't ever coming back, and I was all alone, I decided that I was going to put all of that behind me and forget about his existence. That is why I lied, why I told you that he died. It was to protect us from the past and any future hurt – just bury him, in our minds and in our hearts."

Rachel's eyes started tearing up. She remembered only bits and pieces about her father, but at the time it was only she and her mother. *That* she remembered full well.

"That's when the walls came up and the prickly thorns started to appear. I had to protect myself against any future hurt, and I told myself that I was protecting you as well in this way. I also promised myself that I would never trust another man as long as I live. I never realised the full impact all this had on you. I never gave it any thought. I was so determined to protect us against the world, and to be financially independent. That was all that mattered to me, and you, my dear Rachel, got lost in it and at the same time stuck in it." Rose stopped abruptly and blew her nose.

Rachel wanted to go off again, but decided against it. She knew that in order to understand and to ultimately put this behind her, she had to listen, and not talk.

"You know when your husband Dean died..."

"What does Dean have to do with any of this? Why are you dragging him into this?" Rachel's face started to turn red again and she felt her heart beating faster.

"Just wait, listen Rachel. It will become clear in a minute. Just give me a chance," Rose almost begged Rachel to let her finish.

"Okay, Mother. Go ahead." She promised herself to keep quiet this time.

"When Dean died, you probably felt like your whole world came to an end, that you are all alone in this world. I know you had Lily, but losing a man is like losing yourself. You have to start all over again, without him. It was the same for me, except that my husband didn't die, he just up and left. Leaving me, and leaving you, his own flesh and blood!"

Rachel looked shocked and hurt. This is not new to her, but hearing her mother explain it to her, like that! That made all the difference and she felt that she finally understood everything.

"I never realised that his abandonment had such an effect on you. You always looked so strong and proud;

like nothing could ever touch you, and nothing did, not even me."

"Oh, Rachel, my dear Rachel." Rose stood up and hugged Rachel who was already on her feet and in tears.

"I am so sorry, so, so sorry. How can I ever make it right, make it go away?" she sighed and both women cried softly. Releasing years of pain, years of resentment and years of misunderstandings.

"I too have to apologise, Mother. I never realised, nor understood what you went through. I was only preoccupied with my own hurt and resentment and anger over being lied to. I was only concerned with me believing that lie and missing out on having a father. But now, fully realising what he had done, I ask myself, do I honestly want him for a father? I think it's best that I give up my search and let him stay buried. I only wanted his love and approval, but now, it seems to me, that all I really want, is *your* love. Your love and approval of me," Rachel's voice broke, and again the two women stood there hugging and crying all their troubles away.

"I love you Rachel. You are my daughter. I am so proud of you and especially of how you are coping with Dean's death. I know I don't say that a lot, ha-ha, but I have always loved you and I always will. You and Lily Anne. You are my whole world!" she said with deep affection. Lily walked in and immediately stopped in her tracks.

"What's going on here? Are you all right?" she asked with great concern. Both mother and daughter laughed while drying the welcome tears from their eyes. They both beckoned her to come closer.

"Don't worry, Lily, everything is all right,

everything," Rachel said with a big smile on her freckled face while she gently stroked Lily's shiny black hair. She felt so much love at that moment, it made her heart swell with peace and happiness. Rose's blue eyes mirrored the exact same feelings. She finally found her peace and her clock was still ticking!

David was right... again.

CHAPTER 5: PRECIOUS SIGHT

Bethany stepped into the dimly lit church, feeling her way with her trusty walking stick. She knew the church would likely be empty, seeing that it was a weekday and she came here almost every day.

She listened attentively – that's what she did these days – in order to corroborate what she sensed at that moment. Lately, she accepted that she had to rely on those senses telling her what her eyes could not. Satisfied that she was the only one there, she tapped her way to the front of the church.

She knelt down and while holding her shiny cross, she said her daily prayers. She spoke so softly, no one would be able to hear. That didn't matter, Bethany thought, her prayers only needed to reach one pair of ears.

She believed that when they do, He would hear and He would suddenly act! She believed that so strongly, it sometimes felt that He was there with her, whispering something that she just couldn't hear. How ironic. She was blind, not deaf!

"Beth," she heard a familiar voice behind her. "I thought that was you. Here, let me help you." She stood up and was aiming for the candles, but she let the priest lead her to them.

By this time he knew her little ritual – she came in and prayed; then she would light two candles, one for her father and one for her mother; then finally, she would sit in one of the front pews and just get lost in the endless peace and quiet.

"How are you, Bethany?" he asked softly. Ever since the accident, he took a special interest in her. He knew it wasn't easy going through what she went through these past few years. The thing that amazed him the most, and kept him immensely interested in her, was her thankfulness and gracefulness. It was the first time in his life that he witnessed this type of reaction to such tragic events.

"I'm fine, thank you, Father. How are you?" she asked politely

"You know, everything is in God's hands. My wellbeing too. Have you heard from your sister?" he asked with a concerned voice.

Bethany moved her walking stick from one side to the other and leaned back against the hard wooden backrest. She liked Father Frances, he was very protective of her, but in a way that didn't smother her. He was also genuinely concerned about her, but again not overly concerned. He had a natural tendency to balance the two, perfectly.

"I haven't heard from her in a while. I think she is having one of those spells again, where she pulls back and doesn't talk to anyone. I'm giving her time and space to sort things out for herself. I believe that one day, she'll accept what happened and move on,"

Bethany answered patiently and moved her stick once more from one side to the other.

Father Frances took note, he knew all too well how much she valued her quiet time in the church.

"Are you going to visit your parents today?" he asked with a tangible gentleness in his voice.

"Yes, Father, I feel it's time again." He could detect a little sadness in her voice and his heart went out to her. Poor child, he thought and shook his grey head.

"You have yourself a good day now, you hear," he finally said and patted her lily-white hand. "I'll see you tomorrow, Bethany." He slowly stood up and waited for her goodbye.

"Thank you, Father Frances. I hope you have a heavenly day," she said and smiled mischievously. He smiled too and he felt a little better about leaving her. Bethany could hear his slow footsteps fade away as he walked towards his 'office'.

Alone again, she thought. Her blindness brought a lot of alone time – friends stayed away out of pity. They didn't know what to say half of the time, or even how to behave around her. As if she wasn't the same person anymore.

Except for her sister; she came to visit regularly and always insisted that Beth move in with her. Bethany refused every time, because it would feel like the very last shred of her independence would be taken away then. She needed her independence, every last bit of it, otherwise she would feel completely disabled. AND she did not like that, being blind was bad enough!

The abundant alone time also deepened her faith and trust in God. If it wasn't for that, she would have gone mad and she would have been trapped in endless anger and grief. She learned to accept her 'condition' –

she called it that because she felt that it was only temporary. The doctors basically said it, in so many words. So even though it limited her usual social activities and ultimately changed her lifestyle tremendously, she still accepted it. In her heart she knew that those Ears would hear!

Feeling calmly content again, Bethany took her trusty white walking stick and tap-tapped her way out of the darkish church into the bright sunlight. She knew it was bright, because she could feel its welcoming warmth on her pale skin. She enjoyed that, because it felt like, should she stand in it long enough, she just might catch a glimmer of something, so bright was it.

She decided to go to the large cemetery next. It was close to the church and she knew it was five blocks to the left. She could hear the busy street next to her and the voices of fellow pedestrians passing her by.

She could tell when she neared the familiar cemetery – a very jovial street vendor named Joey, always greeted her in his thick Italian accent. She could also smell his mouth-watering hotdog stand a block away.

"Buongiorno, Bettini. How are you today?" Joey asked cheerfully as he helped her around his hotdog stand.

"Good morning, Joey. I'm fine, thank you, and you?" Bethany asked spiritedly. She enjoyed chatting to Joey. He was always so happy to see her and so easy-going. She felt completely at ease in his presence, because he had no pretences – Joey was just Joey, nothing more, nothing less!

"I'm fantastico, always magnifico! Come, let me give you a nice hotdog, one with everything!" He started to fill one of the white rolls and just as he promised, stuffed it with everything: fried onions, tomato relish, mustard...

"Thank you, Joey. You truly are one of a kind," Bethany said as he carefully placed the messy hotdog and a paper napkin in her cupped hands.

Bethany stood there next to his warm stand and ate her delicious hotdog as respectably as she possibly could.

"Is good, si?" Joey asked enthusiastically and watched appreciatively as she ate the overfilled hotdog with great enjoyment.

"It's good, Joey, as always. Thanks again!" Bethany answered while she cleaned her face with the paper napkin.

"Your face is good, Bettini. Here, give me the napkin. I throw it away for you." Joey took the smeared napkin and dropped it in the trash can.

"Grazie, Joey. You are so kind. How is business?" she asked genuinely interested.

"Eh, business is good. Hotdogs very popular," he answered enthusiastically.

"And your family, are they well?" she asked again.

"Mia famiglia is good, also fantastico!" Bethany knew he loved his family very much – he did all this for them.

"I have to get going now, Joey, but I will see you again, or should I say I will hear you again." They both laughed at their little inside joke. She turned around and held her stick in front of her.

"Arrivederci, Bettini cara. Have a good day," he said buoyantly and waved as she walked away tapping the level pavement.

After a few more steps, Bethany entered the lonely

cemetery through the two big black iron gates. She memorised the path leading to the two well-known graves that she wanted to visit. She appreciated the well-kept, even footpath and she could hear the tapping of her stick clearly.

It gradually became quiet all around her, she could almost feel the quiet. She could also feel the warm rays of the sun filtering through the tall trees. When she stepped off the path onto the soft springy grass, someone grabbed her arm and pulled her aside. She almost fell from the sudden movement, but a strong hand held her soft hand tightly, preventing her from falling.

Bethany was still busy collecting herself, when she heard a man's voice.

"Are you all right?" he asked very concerned. She started straightening herself, when the man's voice repeated his question with even more concern – she could almost feel his concern. How strange, she thought.

"Yes, yes, I'm fine, thank you," she finally answered him and with a deep frown she asked, "What happened?" She felt those same hands as he placed her walking stick into her searching hands. She noticed how big they felt. She could also feel the strength in them.

"You were about to step into that open grave, and I pulled you away just in time. Are you sure you are all right?" he asked for a third time.

"Yes, thank you. This is going to sound strange, but I lost my direction. Could you please take me to my parents' graves?" she asked with uncertainty, she had no other choice.

"All right, it's the least I could do for handling you

so roughly, but I just wanted to prevent you from falling into that open grave." Huh, what a thought! Bethany shuddered at the thought, not because it was a grave, but how on earth would she have gotten out!

"Thank heavens you were here," she said, her voice filled with gratitude.

"I'm David, by the way, and you're welcome. Why don't you give me their names, and I will lead you to them?" he asked softly.

"I'm Bethany. David, what a handsome name. What are the odds that you, David, and my dearly departed father shared the same name?" she asked, sharing her wondering thoughts.

"I suppose it would be the same odds that brought me here, at this very moment. So I'm looking for a David...?" David asked intrigued by this woman who seemed so different from the others.

"It's David and Mari Winstead. It's easy to find. Just look for a headstone shaped like a heart," Bethany said softly. David could see sorrow written all over her pale face.

David walked in the direction Bethany told him, leading her with her hand tucked beneath his elbow. Sure enough, he soon found the heart-shaped headstone and read their names to her. Satisfied that it's the right one, he decided to stand aside under one of the leafy green trees, giving her privacy.

Bethany knelt down and lovingly touched the familiar heart-shaped headstone. She may not be able to see it, but she knew the grey heart with the precious names engraved on it, by heart!

She lost both her parents about two years ago in a horrible car accident. A truck driver, who fell asleep behind the wheel, ended both their lives way too soon.

She missed them so much, every single day. She had such good, loving parents; probably the best, according to her. She came here regularly to visit their graves, their last resting place.

Usually she would just sit and listen to all the memories being played in her head. But today she just wanted to thank them for all their love, their kindness, their support and their guidance. Were it not for all that and for the strong foundation they helped to lay, she would not have coped with her 'condition', the way she did. She would have drowned in it, instead.

"Are you still here, David?" Bethany asked as she got to her feet, her walking stick ready.

"Yes, I am," he answered as he came closer.

"Oh, my goodness!" Bethany exclaimed. How could I be so dense, she asked herself. "I'm sorry," she started, "it would seem that I'm being completely thoughtless. You are probably here to visit someone, same as me. Why would you still be here?" she asked while she touched her head.

David smiled, this smile also reached his light-brown eyes. Bethany certainly was not like other people, and it puzzled him why their paths had crossed. It didn't seem like she needed help, so he kept on wondering.

"Why indeed?" he thought aloud, and only then realised that she heard him.

"So, are you visiting someone?" Bethany asked again, also looking for answers. She did not believe in coincidences. There must be a reason for everything, you may not know it, but there is. That's what she believed.

Why then, was this stranger placed on her path, she wondered silently. Maybe he could shed some light on that, because he didn't come across as ordinary – there was something different about him. She could feel it, and lately, she had learnt to pay more attention to her gut feeling. She also learned to attach more value to what she felt.

"No," David decided to tell the truth, as he always did. "I turned in here, thinking it was a park, but to my unexpected surprise, it turned out to be a cemetery that held such beauty. I was just about to leave, when I saw you. I also saw the open grave and I thought to myself, it was lucky that I did!"

"I'm glad that you did. That would not have been any fun, falling into an open grave. Not being able to see anything. How would I have gotten out?" she asked, again shuddering at the mere thought.

"About that. Were you always blind?" David asked tentatively. Bethany started walking towards a wooden bench she remembered, feeling her way with her trusty old stick. David followed and got seated next to her with his trustworthy backpack next to him.

"About a year ago, my sister and I were also, ironically, in a car accident. Where my parents lost their lives, we walked away alive, but I walked away blind." She looked sad, David thought. How tragic for her – losing both her parents, and then being blinded.

"The doctors are positive that I will possibly see again, they just can't say when. But I believe, firmly and strongly, that I will see again and it won't take years and years. This is going to sound strange, but I pray everyday to God, I speak into His Ear, for Him to restore my vision. That is why I call it my 'condition', because I know in my heart, that it's only temporary."

David was glad that she could not see his face, there was pure astonishment written all over it. Usually, *he* was the one to inspire and help people, but it would seem that this amazing woman did not need any help.

"You said that you and your sister were in an accident. What happened to her?" he asked softly with concern in his voice.

"Sarah? She was extremely lucky. She walked away with only scrapes and bruises, but that's where the good news ended. What she did walk away with, was severe guilt." Bethany shook her head in sympathy.

"I feel for her. I may not be able to see her beautiful face, but I can hear it every time she speaks. I can feel the atmosphere getting heavier when she comes to visit." Bethany paused, reflecting on what she just said and on her own feelings about the accident.

David felt more and more ashamed. Here comes this blind woman filled with so much faith, that she could see for the both of them, he thought exasperated. He shook his head.

What did *he* do?

When faced with his own struggle in life, he did not turn to God, he did not deepen his faith like Bethany did.

No. He, David, ran.

That was what he did, he RAN!

And he was still running. Like it or not, he was still running as fast as he could!

"Are you still here, David?" Bethany asked as the prolonged silence reached her thoughts. She could feel the sun warming her tawny, straight hair and slightly burning her pale soft skin.

She knew it was time to go and seeing that, or perhaps hearing that, David was all of a sudden very quiet, she thought it a good time to go their separate ways again.

Bethany rose slowly and tried to feel for David's arm. She touched something that felt like a large backpack, and then traced it with her fingers till she finally found his muscular arm. She stopped and again spoke his name.

He looked up, not feeling his usual friendly, pleasant self and saw this angel-like face before him that he will probably never forget. It's not just the face; it's this whole being that kept radiating this incredible, inherent good, like a super-sun!

"I'm here," he finally said, knowing that in a day or two he would be his good, old self again. He just needed to figure some things out for himself. To look at some of the truths that he has been avoiding.

"I have to go," she said gently, "my sister is coming over this afternoon and I have to get back. It was nice meeting you, David." She held out her soft hand. David took it. Her hand felt so warm and sincere in his, he almost teared up.

This day was beginning to take its toll on him.

"It was nice meeting you too," he said with sincerity. "I hope you enjoy your sister's visit, and I also hope that God will hear your prayers, Bethany." He was just able to get that last bit out.

"Goodbye, David. Take care of yourself, and remember, you are not alone." Those were her last words to him, and he could see her disappearing between the headstones as he sat there completely overcome by emotion.

Bethany tapped-tapped her way home like she always did, but she felt completely different. She felt so alive, and everything around her, felt so alive. It was like every sound, every smell was amplified, even the way things felt – it was like they were vibrating with life! And on top of all that, she felt like she realised things that she had forgotten.

She might be blind, but she was still able to help someone. It felt like this person needed it more than she did, and she was so glad that she was able to do just that!

She entered her ground floor apartment feeling elated; it was good to be home, her home. She moved about in high spirits, preparing for her sister's visit. She really wanted to 'see' her and to talk to her like sisters should.

After her parents' deaths, she valued family even more and she wanted to make every visit, every moment, count! She didn't want any regrets, and that was also one of the many reasons that she wanted desperately to help Sarah get past her guilt – her consuming remorse.

A bit tired, but pleased, Bethany got comfortable on her soft sofa and slowly leaned back her buxom body. She closed her eyes and just listened to the quiet which folded around her like a familiar blanket. Her mind was quiet, so quiet and peaceful...

She heard a knock, and the front door opened. She opened her dark brown eyes, and asked the dreamlike shadow: "Sarah, is that you?"

CHAPTER 6: PLEASE FORGIVE ME

Sarah sat quiet as a mouse while she had her nails done at her favourite beauty parlour. She preferred this salon, because the girls working there would only strike up a conversation if that was what the client wanted.

She didn't feel like talking that particular morning and was therefore glad that Molly, the beautician who usually did her nails, just went about her business, and respected her silence.

Molly was very intuitive that way and could sense that it was one of those days, when the world and your personal issues just weighed you down. She felt sorry for Sarah, and she wished that she could find the right words that would simply lift her spirits.

But the right words did not come, so they sat in silence with only the background music and neighbouring voices poking at their mutual silence.

With her new nails, a shining brilliant red, she thanked Molly and left the busy parlour to go look for a nice cup of coffee. She knew of this little coffee shop which was well-known for its cosy atmosphere. She then decided to walk the short distance to 'Café Coffee Beans' and also to feel the warm, yellow sun on her tanned legs.

She had another photo shoot that weekend and thus had to look her best. She already visited the gym early that morning, and she was trying to get everything done before that afternoon. Sarah was going to visit her sister that afternoon, and it was very important to her.

Her sister, Sarah thought, and got that familiar sad look on her pretty face. That was a whole different story, one she desperately tried to get away from, but she could not. Every time she saw her, there was that clear ugly painful reminder of the car accident she had caused which left her dear sister, Bethany, blinded, quite possibly for life!

What was she supposed to do, she asked herself for the hundredth time. She was stupid, maybe even reckless, and young, and at that time all she wanted in life was to have fun. Fun, fun, fun. She was young and that was what young people were supposed to do – have fun!

That all changed after the accident. She went from being a carefree, young, fun-seeking girl to a serious Sam with serious issues. It felt like the outside world did not matter as much; all that mattered was this terrible guilt that simply would not go away! *She* had to live with the daily self-reproach and the enormous guilt for the rest of her life. And the remorse she felt in her heart, grew steadily every time she saw Beth.

Sarah tried hard to still have fun, seeing that she was still young and a model, but she must admit that after the accident, it felt so fake, so empty, like she wasn't that fun-loving-girl anymore. It rather felt like she was using that part of herself to mask the part that was overrun with guilt and remorse.

Seeing the sign of the little coffee shop brought her back to the present where, ironically, everything seemed so easy and so simple. Her deep blue eyes read the sign 'Café Coffee Beans', before she entered the dark red and chocolate coloured shop. She walked straight to the cluttered counter and ordered the largest size Americano.

When she took her pink wallet out to pay, Sarah unknowingly dropped something very valuable.

She waited five minutes in the pleasant atmosphere and then collected her tall coffee mug, some sweetener and only a little bit of milk. She was lucky enough to get one of the cosy corners and she immediately claimed it for herself.

She loved this specific corner, because it was out of the way and she could do her favourite thing – people watching. She enjoyed doing that, because you get so many interesting people and the way they differed from each other, always intrigued her!

Sarah was so absorbed by this one couple, she was completely unaware of the stranger standing by her round table, calling softly, trying to get her attention.

"Is this yours?" The man's voice finally penetrated her focused mind, and Sarah turned to look at the man calling her.

Before her stood a tall, bulky middle-aged man with dark brown hair, complimented by a dark brown beard. He was holding with an outstretched arm, the valuable item she had dropped unknowingly.

"Is this yours?" he asked again with a surprisingly gentle voice, considering his sheer size. It was a photograph of her late parents which she always carried with her.

"Yes, OMG, thank you so much," she said relieved and very glad as she took the photo from him. Their hands touched lightly, briefly.

"Where did you find it?" she asked concerned and at the same time with gratitude.

He looked with his light-brown eyes at the beautiful blonde before him. She had a very delicate face, with the most beautiful big blue eyes; they looked so gentle. They matched her gentle, feminine manner, but he also saw a certain kind of strength lurking in them.

"You dropped it by the counter. I was lucky enough to see the photo fall out of your handbag," he answered in a sincere voice.

"Thanks again. You're a lifesaver. This photograph means a lot to me, it's very near and dear to me," Sarah said as she looked at it with sadness and at the same time, with a loving happiness.

"I can see that. I'm David, by the way. Are they your parents?" he asked softly, gently; his eyes filled with compassion.

"Oh, gosh. Where are my manners? I'm Sarah. Won't you please sit down and let me buy you a coffee? It's the least I can do!" Her voice sounded like little bells; so clear and light and also gentle, like her, David thought as he took his heavy backpack off.

"I accept your offer, but can you buy me a nice cup of tea instead?" he asked while he took a seat opposite Sarah. She looked at his worn, stuffed backpack as he placed it beside him. She wondered what that was all about, because he didn't look like a homeless person, but he also didn't strike her as the hiking type.

"I'll order you some tea," she said while she stood

up. "Do you have any preferences?" He looked at her lovely face, and smiled.

"No, but I do like my tea hot and black. Oh, and sweet, very sweet!" he answered with a boyish smile. "Remember your photograph," he added. Sarah smiled, her red lips forming a perfect frame around her lily-white teeth.

"I'll remember, thank you," she answered appreciatively and walked over to the busy counter for a refill – she loved her coffee – and tea for her new friend.

To David's surprise, Sarah returned with his hot tea and little sugar packets, and a brown paper bag with the coffee shop's name printed on the side.

"I got you something extra, seeing that you're a backpacker, *and* you found my precious keepsake," she said smiling as she got comfortable. David watched her attentively as she arranged their drinks and the something extra on the table. He could hear her delicate bangles as they lightly jingled against each other.

She suddenly looked up, straight at him, with those big blue eyes.

"You asked me earlier about the photo, it is indeed my parents, but unfortunately they both died two years ago in a fatal car accident." Her gentle eyes looked so sad, David thought, as she looked at the photo.

"This is one of just a few mementos I still have of them." She took a sip of her strong coffee and started fiddling with the empty sugar packets.

"That's a sad day for anyone, to lose a parent is bad enough, but to lose both at the same time, that is sheer tragedy," David said as he broke off a piece of his giant carrot-and-nut muffin and put it in his mouth.

"This is really good," he said smiling in an effort to lighten the mood.

"I'm glad you like it. Coffee Beans is well-known for their tasty baked goods. That's why I got one for my dear sister as well – I know she likes them, and of course there's her sweet tooth!" her voice sounding like little bells again. They both sat in silence, each enjoying their hot beverage.

"You mentioned your sister, is it just the two of you? What I mean is, it's good to have someone, especially now, and not be all alone," he asked cautiously, yet softly.

"Yes, it's just me and Beth now, thank God for her. She is like my rock, my anchor. I was the unstable one, particularly after my parents' death, but every time she was the one that brought me back, time after time – she brought me back..." she stared off into the distance for a moment, and then continued.

"Which is ironic if you think about it. She was blinded by a car crash I had caused. This was a year after we lost our parents." Her lovely face got sullen. She pulled her full lips into an embittered line across her face.

David looked at her with so much compassion and understanding, it surprised her. Sarah expected something else, but not eyes filled with so much compassion and sincerity, it left her speechless.

"That must be a terrible burden to carry around," David finally said in his usual gentle manner. Her blue eyes came to rest on his worn backpack.

"You can't even begin to imagine. It's like waking up every day with a giant backpack on your back crammed with cast-iron bricks of guilt, cast-iron bricks of self reproach and cast-iron bricks of remorse. And the worst part, you get to take yours off as you please, but I don't! I have to carry mine for the rest of my life!" She sounded defeated, like she just got a death sentence.

David felt so sorry for her, and once again, his heart went out to her. It seemed so unfair that this beautiful, young woman had this heavy burden inside of her, weighing her down bit by bit, every single day of her life!

They heard a loud noise coming from the coffee counter. Someone was using a machine to make some sort of drink which was clanking loudly. This gave David time to finish his giant muffin and to be inspired. He savoured the last bite of his carrot-and-nut muffin, because it was so good.

It was clear to him that Sarah needed to forgive herself, urgently. Otherwise, she would be completely destroyed by the immense guilt she felt. Sarah was still playing with the little white sugar packet when she suddenly stopped to read a message printed on it. She did not notice the small blue letters until then.

"'Very little is needed to make a happy life; it is all within yourself, in your way of thinking', Marcus Aurelius," she read the message aloud. David thought that this was his chance to help her realise that she needed to forgive herself; the sooner, the better!

"Sarah, do you know what that means?" he asked while looking at her confused expression. He could see clearly that she did not comprehend what she had just read.

"I think I do," she answered hesitantly, unsure of her answer.

"You told me that the accident, caused by you, has left your sister blind, possibly for life. There is nothing you can do about that; it happened and you're obviously punishing yourself for that everyday. I also assume that you want forgiveness from your sister..." he started to explain patiently, before Sarah interrupted him.

"That's the best of all, she doesn't hold a grudge or blame me or anything of the sort. She forgave me from day one. She believes that one day she'll be able to see again. I think that's why I blame myself to the max, because she already forgave me and she was never, ever angry, not even once, not with me anyway. It just makes it so much harder," she said disheartened.

"It's obvious to me. You need forgiveness. You want forgiveness so that your heavy burden may be lifted. Then, and only then, can you live again, and be Sarah again. The thing is, you need to forgive yourself, really forgive yourself, and try to move on. Everyday, really try to move on and put the car accident and its tragic consequences behind you, once and for all." David spoke softly and sincerely, and then suddenly remembered the strength he saw in her big blue eyes.

"You have the strength you need inside of you. It is all within yourself – you remember the quote you read? Have the courage to find your own strength, and then use that strength to forgive yourself. It takes tremendous strength to forgive such seemingly unforgivable acts with such tragic consequences. But lucky for you, Sarah, you have all the strength you need, right there," he pointed towards her heart, "to do just that!" He took a deep breath when he finished and gave her an encouraging, bearded smile.

"Hi, Sarah," they both turned to look at the thin, young man standing next to their wooden table. "I thought that was you. How are you?" the pleasant, young man greeted Sarah, and gave David a quick smile.

"Hi, Rick. This is David; David, Rick," she introduced the two men and got up. "Just give me a minute, Rick. I also have to get going, but I will see you outside?" she kindly asked Rick and waited until he left, before she turned back to David.

"It was so nice meeting you, David," she said in her bell-like voice and started to get her things together as she spoke. "I enjoyed our chat, even if it was heavy hearted, but the advice you gave me is golden. I will definitely give it serious thought," she said with her lovely red smile.

"It was nice meeting you too, and I sincerely hope that things work out for you, Sarah, and that you get your much needed absolution." David watched her very feminine hands as they gently collected her belongings and also the brown paper bag.

"You know, David, I just shockingly realized that I know nothing about you. We only spoke about me, my issues and my life!" She looked at him inquiringly. David just smiled and without answering extended his hand, which Sarah took appreciatively.

Rick tapped against the window pane and pointed with a bony finger at his wristwatch. Sarah gave him a smile and a little wave, as if to say 'I'm coming, hold your horses.'

"Well then, David, I suppose this is it, and I too hope that you and your backpack get to where it is you want to be. Goodbye, dear David," she said with a big smile and a quick wink and then hurried to the young, impatient man waiting outside!

David watched her beautiful wavy blonde hair as she walked away. He could still hear the little bells in her voice mixed with the jingling of her delicate bangles.

All that was left of their encounter were their empty mugs, little brown crumbs, and her sweet perfume which reminded him of a long ago spring filled with wild flowers and playful fluttering butterflies...

"Hi, Rick, thanks for waiting," Sarah said as she joined him outside the coffee shop.

"Who was that?" Rick asked with a slight hint of suspicion in his voice.

He doesn't like it when people take advantage of her gentle nature, and thus sees himself as her protector. Almost like a big brother, but in his heart, he wished that they could be more.

"David is just a guy who found my treasured photo, and as a 'thank you', I bought him a cup of tea. He's actually a very nice guy, with insight that would astound you." She answered his strict question with gentle words, because she knew that her words would put his suspicious mind at ease, and to lighten his mood, she quickly added a question of her own.

"Did you get those shots you were looking for?"

Rick's face immediately started to brighten and he spoke excitedly about the excellent shots that he was lucky enough to get. His photographer-hands eagerly joined in the conversation as he gesticulated exactly how he got different shots – "it's all about the angles," he said almost breathlessly.

"Do you want to see them? Now, maybe?" he asked unexpectedly.

Sarah looked at him with adoration, and smiled. She liked seeing this side of him, when he spoke of his one true passion, photography. He got carried away so often, you had to blow a horn or something just to get his attention.

"Yes, of course, now is fine. I want to visit Beth this afternoon, but there's plenty of time to go with you and admire your art, because it is pure art," she said with those familiar little bells ringing in her gentle voice.

Looking at his photographs was like watching pieces of art hanging in a gallery. Rick had a lot of pride in his work, because it was his greatest passion and he was very professional when it came to his work. Sarah always enjoyed looking through his photos, not only because they were extremely professional, but they also showed his raw talent.

She listened intently as he feverishly explained his vision for his next exhibition. He spoke of 'urban living' and 'urban recreation' as his theme and how he tried to capture the very essence of that in his shots.

As she looked at each individual photograph, she saw that he once again succeeded in depicting his theme, his vision, through his extremely graphic and lively photographs. Another thing that she appreciated, was his uncanny ability to make you feel that you could reach in and touch the skateboard as it hurled through the air!

Sarah was so transfixed by his photos, she completely lost track of time.

The unexpected rumbling of her tummy brought her attention back to the present moment. Only then did she realise how hungry she actually was. Rick heard it too and laughed.

"Yeah, it's hard being a model..." And he laughed some more. "Would you like a sandwich? I'm going to make me one," Rick asked while pulling his mouth in such a way, it reminded Sarah of an elf. His face always reminded her of an elf, but in a good way, and that was just one more reason why she liked Rick so much.

"Yes, thank you, but it'll have to be a quick one. I still have to travel across town to get to Beth's place," she answered in her usual gentle, feminine manner.

"How is Bethany?" Rick asked with concern as they ate their stuffed sandwiches.

"She is doing great. It seems that she is getting more independent every time I see her. I'm very happy for her. She can at least have some normalcy, but I still hope that the doctors are right in their prognosis – that she will see again!" Her voice broke a little, and that lovely face got sullen again.

Rick folded his hands around her soft, tanned hands and looked into her sad, blue eyes. He could feel his heart contract a little, he so wanted to console her like a real man, her man, but he was afraid that it might scare her off and he would never see her again. He could not bear the thought of losing her, and so, he once again settled for being the big brother she never had.

"I'm sure the doctors are right, and Beth will have her sight back. Forget about that horrible accident, and stop punishing yourself. It happened. You were young. Rather remember that you still have your sister, and that one day soon, she will see again!" Rick emphasised every word and let them flow from his heart.

She looked up at his boyish face and gave him a brave smile. He could always make her feel better, and things didn't seem so lost, so beyond repair then. She started gathering her girly things and thanked him for the lovely sandwich.

"You are one of a kind, Rick," she said with her red lips pulled in a brilliant smile again.

"Thank you for understanding, for understanding me, and for being there whenever I need you – saying the right things, doing the right things. Yip, you are one of a kind!"

She remembered to take her brown paper bag as well, then gave Rick a slight kiss on his angular cheek, touching his tawny straight hair lightly.

The cab's loud honking put an abrupt end to their rare moment, and they hastily said their goodbyes. Rick even wished her best of luck with her visit.

It was a good long distance to her sister's apartment, and the cab ride over, gave her the perfect opportunity to think things over. Rick's words still rang in her ears, "stop punishing yourself." Was she really doing that? Punishing herself? It seemed so clear now.

She knew that she was overwhelmed by her own guilt and remorse over the accident. She did not, however, realise that it turned into a whip that she used to punish herself with daily.

David was right, she needed to forgive herself, rather urgently, otherwise – at the rate she was going – there would be nothing left, no Sarah, just an empty space where there once lived a happy, young, fun-loving girl.

Did she really have the courage and the strength he talked about, she thought as she watched the different buildings flash by.

After a while, they drove slowly past a city bus and something caught her eye. On the side of the bus, she read a popular slogan used by one of the candidates running for mayor.

"The time is now," she read it slowly over and over

as they waited at the red light.

It felt as though it was a message for her, and it was trying to tell her something, to make her realise something... In her heart she knew what that was, the whole day hinted at it, almost incessantly.

It was time.

It was time for her, Sarah Winstead, to forgive herself, once and for all, at long last, forgive herself.

As they neared her destination, she felt like something started to give way inside of her. It felt like an invisible hand was slowly starting to chip away at her iron-cast guilt. Guilt which became such a part of her, and of her life, it completely consumed her without her even noticing.

By the time they reached Beth's place, she felt calm, like a very still pond, not even a ripple. She also felt light, lighter than usual, almost like a feather, but not quite.

Sarah smiled, an emancipated smile, when she climbed out of the yellow cab and paid the young Asian driver, her delicate bangles jingled again as they slid down her arm to her slim wrist.

She took a moment, and then briskly walked the last few steps to Bethany's ground floor apartment. She knocked three times making sure that Bethany would hear them, and then opened the wooden front door slowly, purposefully.

"Sarah, is that you?" she heard her sister's voice ask as she entered her dusky apartment.

"Hi, Bethany!" she greeted Beth in a chirpy tone of voice. Her sister looked confused and she kept blinking her eyes.

Sarah walked over to the large windows and pulled the thin curtains back. She could see better then and was on her way to Bethany's seat, when Beth asked her to go stand against the window.

Bethany was squinting her dark brown eyes and still looked flurried.

"Is something wrong, Beth? You look confused." Sarah watched with great concern as Bethany stood up, and started blinking again.

Her dark brown eyes suddenly widened and with a shaky voice she answered Sarah.

"I see a dreamlike shadow, Sarah. An apparition, I think. Move around a little," she instructed Sarah as she tried to unravel the puzzling image she saw.

Then it dawned on her.

She wasn't imagining some holy apparition as she had thought, nor was she seeing a ghost. She was in fact SEEING her sister.

She was seeing Sarah!

"I can see you!" she shouted. "Oh my God, Sarah, I can see you!" her voice broke as she started crying – sobbing louder and louder.

Sarah raced to her side and hugged Bethany like she hasn't hugged her in a long time. They both cried, tears of joy and tears of immense relief streaming down their faces.

"It's a miracle! I am so, so happy for you, Bethany!" Sarah whispered in Beth's ear, and at the same time felt the very last bit of guilt and remorse leave her heart, only to be replaced by some much needed love and joy!

Bethany started laughing and Sarah could see pure happiness all over her face, even her eyes, her beautiful dark brown eyes looked like they were gleaming with intense joy.

The doctors were right, her sister – Bethany – was

also right acting her unwavering faith.
  She can see again!

CHAPTER 7: HER NAME, WAS GRACE

David was still looking in the direction Bethany had walked off long after she had left. He was still reeling from their encounter, from meeting that amazing human being, and from the true, touching words she spoke.

"You are not alone," he repeated her moving words.

Just four little words, yet so profound.

It stirred something in him, deep inside. He needed to hear those four little words at that specific moment, he realised. He knew instinctively that it wasn't just her words, it was someone else's words that were spoken through Bethany.

Thank God for Bethany. She had set things in motion, and she didn't even know it!

He turned his head to look at the many graves before him. To think, all these people had lives, each one very important to that person, and each one with its own unique struggle or struggles in life.

Sometimes he wondered whether it was really worth it. Was it?

His attention floated back to his own life, back to his own personal struggle in life. He remembered how it all began.

He was a young man when he arrived at the monastery, so full of life, so full of hope, and with a deep desire to help people and to change their lives.

At first, it all went well, better than expected. He learned about God, about His mercy and His love, about faith, and how you cannot live without it, without Him.

But then, after a while, he started to see things. Things he did not want to see, things he could not comprehend. Things he could not change as a priest, not even with his God.

As a priest, he saw so much hurt and pain and despair in people, and in the world around him, it had left him feeling helpless, almost hopeless. Not even to mention the level of anger and hate he came across.

He found it hard to believe that people could feel that way, be that way! What made it even worse, was the fact that his priesthood, and his precious faith, could not do a damn thing for all of those people, those lost souls.

He started to resent his faith, his priesthood. He also, inadvertently, started to resent God.

How could God, Almighty, just sit there on his Golden Throne, and do nothing? How could He just allow all of that hurt, all of that pain, all of that anger, all of that hatred, to destroy the human race and the world we lived in?

And how could He just allow it to continue, day in and day out, destroying all that we love, all that we hold near and dear to ourselves?

It was then that he, David – a priest, no more –

decided to leave the monastery. To leave all his teachings behind, to leave his Faith behind, and to leave even God Himself behind.

He could not bear to believe in something and someone that would just allow His creation to be brought to ruin. That life altering decision he had made, led to another life changing decision.

He wasn't happy about how God did things, or should he rather say, not do things. It seemed that He did not do anything, so David decided to go at it alone, and do God's work.

It was time to help people, all those poor souls, and to change their lives one way or another...

He looked at the weather-beaten graves again; they seemed so cold and lonely as they stuck out of the earth like giant grey fingers. He got up and stretched his long limbs.

Enough time spent with the dead, it was time to get back to the living, he thought.

He picked up his worn backpack and swung it over his broad shoulders. He felt the heavy weight as it settled on his back.

He felt hungry, really hungry. The people-saving business was hard work and it was beginning to take its toll on him, especially on that day.

He did not know it yet, but his day was far from over. There were some more emotional turmoil laying in wait for him, but first, it was time for some much needed nourishment.

David slowly approached the picturesque food-truck which proudly displayed the colours of India – a very bright orange and green. The greatly popular truck was swarming with eager patrons, all wanting a bite to eat, that was, an Indian bite to eat.

David patiently waited and when it was finally his turn, he ordered their famous potato curry with basmati rice and rotis on the side.

As he got his money out to pay, Raj, the familiar owner, shook his head and said in a firm voice, "No, David, it's on the house. You don't pay. I give you burfee too, something sweet."

He gave David a big smile, showing some missing teeth. With his thin brown arms, he passed the folded paper bag to David and gave him a little wink.

"Thank you, Raj. That is extremely kind of you. Thank you and bless you," David said softly as he took the white paper bag and left, weaving through the hungry, eager faces.

David knew Raj. He was a good man and very passionate about his cooking, hence the frightfully busy food truck.

It wasn't always the case. There was a time when Raj almost lost everything, and almost gave up. Then David came along, and unknowingly fired up Raj's passion and his will to live. Raj never looked back, and became a roaring success, almost overnight.

David smiled, a satisfied smile, it felt good helping people, knowingly or unknowingly, and to see them ultimately soar!

He entered a beautiful, lush-green park, an actual park this time, filled with the most vibrant, colourful flowers; the sweet, honey fragrance they gave off, was delightfully pleasing.

David walked under the outstretched, leafy green giants, thankful for their much desired and appreciated shade. He found the perfect spot for him to enjoy his special meal. He made himself comfortable on one of the many wooden benches.

He started unwrapping his bowl of curry and rice, and immediately his nose was filled with a strong spicy aroma which made his mouth water. Raj did not disappoint. As usual he lived up to his promise, David thought after taking his first, savoury bite.

He closed his light-brown eyes, and let every taste explode in his bearded mouth.

Half-way through his delectable meal, he heard kids playing and laughing which is normal, because there was a playground not far from where he sat.

But when he took a closer look, he saw that it was not what he expected.

What he saw, was something amazing, something to marvel at. It was a group of youngsters, teenagers he assumed, that descended upon the sizeable playground.

They ran and jumped on and off every imaginable object they could find. They made acrobatic somersaults as they disembarked from higher structures, they even made them as they ran through the playground. They also swung from any steel bar they could find, no matter the height.

They were so good at performing their daring stunts and their resourceful tricks, they looked like real gymnasts.

He was so completely absorbed by their creative game, he realised that he totally forgot about eating his tasty food. He kept watching their death defying stunts as he finished his spicy meal.

The youngsters did their exciting tricks with such ease, David thought impressed.

He then saw an unexpected flash, but wasn't quite

sure until he saw the thin, tall frame move.

It would seem that David wasn't their only spectator. Armed with his fancy camera, Rick was also there admiring their awe inspiring stunts and was busy catching it all, every move, on film.

David devoured his sweet surprise – his three burfees – faster than he would have liked to.

He enjoyed eating to such a degree, the act of eating has become like a sacred ritual to him, he savoured every mouthful with a thankful heart.

But right then he had to forgo all that, because he felt an inexplicable urge to go and talk to Rick.

David knew by now that these urges or hunches were there for a reason, and it was best, not to ignore them and to act immediately!

With his last bite safely secured in his mouth, he stood up hands full, and walked over to the nearest garbage bin in the direction of where Rick was standing, busy capturing every move. By the time he reached Rick, he was already down to his last roll of film, it would seem.

Just as well, it would appear that the group of youngsters grew tired of the nice playground. They slowly but surely, started to move on to a more challenging, recreational site.

"Hello, again," he greeted Rick carefully not sure what to expect, but even so he continued talking in his normal gentle manner.

"So, you like taking photographs?" he asked sincerely, completely aware of the sheer zeal with which Rick took his photos. He looked like a real professional doing it!

"Oh, it's you," Rick replied as he looked David over distrustfully. "What do you want?" he asked brusquely while capturing two more shots.

David could tell that these shots would come out very special. Rick took great pains in getting the perfect shot *and* at the best possible angle. David had an inkling that his encounter with Rick would be met with a certain amount of resistance, but he chose to plough right through in spite of it.

"The question isn't what I want, it should rather be, what do you want?" Rick looked at him confused as the last teenager left and they were all alone on the deserted, quiet playground.

David knew that it wouldn't be quiet and deserted for long. Once the temperature starts to drop, the moms with their little ones will fill the playground with their laughter and their usual chit-chat.

Rick finally finished putting his equipment away and was able to pay full attention to the stranger's presence and his unusual question.

"What are you talking about? What do you mean it's about what I want?" he asked mildly irritated. What does this man want and what is he doing here, he thought to himself. He didn't want to spoil his good mood and he wasn't about to let the stranger spoil it either, especially not now.

Not after seeing Sarah, and not after taking these rare shots of people in their urban environment, acting so naturally.

David sighed softly and closed his eyes for an instant, then repeated his question with more sincerity and compassion which was also reflected in his light-brown eyes. Rick saw that and his own demeanour relaxed a little bit.

He looked more closely at the tall, well-built fellow before him. Having a photographer's eye, Rick could see that beneath the slightly bushy beard and longer, dark hair wasn't an old man and neither a wild man.

On the contrary, what he saw, was a man who simply radiated tranquility and sincerity mixed with pure compassion.

He thought about his repetitive question and decided to answer it the way he wanted to.

"I got what I wanted. I wanted spectacular photographs for my urban collection, and I got exactly that, thank you." He smiled a self-complacent smile and pushed his edged chin out, which made his very manly Adam's apple even more prominent.

David's smile was an inward one; he knew this game that humans loved to play, all too well.

'To beat around the bush' was just a way to buy yourself some time, more time to avoid looking at the truth. Usually a truth that needed attention, but most humans found that painful.

And funny enough, it was the much needed attention that brought them closure, and relief from their self-imposed prisons of pain and whatever brought on that pain.

"Your urban collection. What's your urban collection?" David decided to play along for now. He knew that at some stage, you have to man-up.

Man-up to the truth.

You have to own up to the truth, your truth.

Rick started to explain about his new photo collection, themed 'urban living' which focused a lot on 'urban recreation'. That was the reason for him being there in the park, taking pictures of the energetic youngsters.

He began to unwind completely and spoke enthusiastically about 'free running', the activities they both had just witnessed. He told David that he enjoyed watching them perform their daring stunts, and of course to take the best possible shots.

"Sometimes I wish that I could do that. To run free like that and do all sorts of crazy, fun stuff. But, you know, at least I can take part through my lens, and give a voice to today's youth – they do say 'a picture is worth a thousand words'."

David listened intently, he felt glad that Rick decided to open up a bit. That was usually the first step towards acknowledging the truth, and he knew that it wouldn't be long now.

"Is your collection complete now?" he asked intrigued while stroking his bushy, brown beard.

Rick began to laugh, his eyes narrowed into two slits, showing off his elf-like face, complete with thin, sandy hair. David couldn't help but stare at Rick's laughing face, at the face that still looked like a young boy's face, complete with smooth skin.

He suddenly stopped laughing, and turned serious again.

"Sorry about that, but I couldn't help myself. I knew exactly what you meant by 'what do I want', but instead of answering it, I chose this. And so, here we stand, discussing my work like we're two professionals, like you're really interested. Right?"

David was surprised by his quick turn-around. He thought that it would take longer for Rick to get to the good stuff – that's how he referred to the truth, sometimes. Because the truth, no matter how you look at it, it was always stuff, and it was always good, hence the good stuff!

The first mom arrived with her little chatty toddler who was bouncing all over the place. She was also expecting another child and therefore she was laboriously arranging herself on a wooden bench. Then she let the little one loose who didn't need any encouragement tackling the playground equipment with great excitement.

David turned his attention back to Rick, back to his last words.

"You know, a lot of people think they know what they want, but they don't. They don't know, because they don't want to look at what it is that they want, what they really want. They choose to ignore it, because most of the time, they think that they can't get what they want, so they ignore it. They tell themselves that they actually want something else, because they feel that the 'something else' is more attainable. And then they forget what it is that they actually want, until something or someone reminds them again, and that can be painful, because you have been living your lie for so long, and now it is time to look at the truth again, whether you want to or not. So which is it?"

David paused for a second while noticing more mothers with small children filling the colourful playground. Then he asked his final question with sheer earnestness in his usual gentle, caring manner.

"Do you have the heart, the guts to do all that? Rick?" David hooked his big thumbs under his backpack's straps but before Rick could say anything, they both heard this loud cacophony coming from Rick's pocket.

David frowned at the loud noise, while Rick took out his small cell phone and excused himself with an "I have to take this."

David stood around while waiting for Rick to finish his intense conversation. The attractive park was bustling with people then, all wanting a piece of this beautiful place and to bask in the glorious summer sun. He so enjoyed watching their happy faces and listening to their lively voices which was filled with laughter, most of the time.

Rick's tone of voice pulled him back to the present moment.

His boyish face looked happy mixed with some weird kind of joyous relief. His whole demeanour seemed relaxed, and at the same time, pleased.

Hmm, he thought and looked down; his light-brown eyes caught a glimpse of Rick's leather camera case. He took a closer look and read Rick's full name, imprinted on the side.

"So, you're Rick Amos..." David remarked as Rick slid his quiet cell phone back into his tight trouser's pocket.

"Yeah, Amos, like in famous," Rick said slowly completely absorbed in thought.

David could see that Rick was someplace else, and decided to cut their meeting short. He said all that he wanted to say, and he felt satisfied enough that Rick did get his message.

"Who knows, maybe one day you will be famous. With your talent and your passion, you'll probably get there in no time!" He concluded their brief encounter with these final words and left.

It took Rick a few minutes to realise that David had left, and he was standing all alone with his favourite companion safely packed away in its black leather case.

His mind was still processing the unexpected and shocking news he had just received. According to Sarah, his best friend in the whole wide world, her sister – Beth – could now all of a sudden, SEE...

He was still standing in the ripples of his mind trying to understand how that was even possible when he got the alert from the cab company that his cab was waiting for him at the park entrance.

So he quickly yielded to the only truth his mind could find: it must have been a miracle!

It was only on the way over there, that he suddenly remembered about David and all the things he had said, especially the part about what he wanted and being truthful about it.

The truth.

Yes, that's the thing.

The truth, he almost thought aloud, and just remembered in time that he wasn't alone in the car.

That was something that gnawed and gnawed at him for a very long time now, until he finally decided to just peek at it, before he gave it a full on stare.

It made him feel uncomfortable at first, but he kept going and going, and to his surprise, it didn't take him that long to look at it with both eyes wide open!

Rick's truth, it would seem, was his intricate feelings for Sarah.

On the one hand, he wanted to be her best friend, but on the other hand, he wanted more than just friendship.

He wanted to share his romantic feelings with her, because he had such deep feelings for her, and he cared so much for his Sarah.

But he was afraid.

He was afraid that first of all, she didn't feel the way he did, and secondly, he felt that why would she – this beautiful, young model – be interested in this Plain

John with his thin drab hair, his big nose, and not even to mention his scrawny physique.

He had thought about this a lot, and that particular day, it would come to a conclusion, one way or another. He could feel it in his gut.

Especially after her phone call, he could feel it even stronger.

Thus, his decision to muster all his strength and all the courage he could find, so he could tell Sarah that he loved her, and cared for her deeply. He also wanted Sarah to be a part of his life.

He wanted her in his life, always.

He thought that it was now or never. He was going to tell her, *and* miracles *do* happen - it would seem! All's well that ends well!

Rick closed his photographer's eyes and just let everything filter through his psyche, through his whole body.

He heard a deafening bang, and felt a shock like he had never felt before, reverberate through his whole thin body.

Then everything went dark...

David heard an extremely loud bang, like a crashing sound as he passed the busy shops on the wide sidewalk. People started running toward the sound, talking excitedly, with eyes wide open.

When he finally turned the corner, he saw what all the commotion was about.

In front of him, he could barely make out that the ugly mangled piece of metal, was actually the remains of a chequered cab.

The black-and-white mangled mess was pushed up

against the massive, shiny grille of a thirty tonne truck.

David looked with utter horror at the chaotic scene before him.

People were running around, screaming, shouting, some were phoning emergency services, some were completely paralysed with fear, and then there were a few brave souls trying to help the badly injured passengers.

David couldn't help but wonder whether they were alive or not.

Judging by the amount of damage done to the cab, he would have concluded that there weren't any survivors.

The frantic screams coming from the panic-stricken truck driver caught his attention.

He was running around like a crazy person trying to help, trying to assess whether the passengers of the mangled wreck were all right. He was in a complete state of shock. Terror was beginning to set in his stark eyes and his sickly-looking mouth.

That was not the only thing that caught David's heightened attention as he tried to pull the driver out of the way.

His intention was to try and calm the panicked driver, but he broke free of David's strong grip, fighting his way back to the wreckage - and that was that.

Probably for the best, David thought, also half in a stupor, because what he saw caught him completely off guard.

It shook him to his very core, which left him unable to help anyone at that moment, let alone himself!

He backed up slowly until he felt a hard, solid, brick wall pressing against his backpack.

He was so dazed, it took him a couple of minutes to

recall what he had just witnessed.

Not only did he see the worst car crash of his entire life, he may very well know one of the occupants of the black-and-white metal wreck.

David closed his dim, light-brown eyes and again saw the black, leather case with the familiar name printed on the side.

It read in gold lettering: RICK AMOS.

He felt completely helpless, unable to help anyone, and dare he say, hopeless. His whole being was brought to an abrupt and complete standstill.

He felt like he had no control any longer, over anything, not even David himself, which was rare.

He felt like everything he had done up until that moment, was all in utter vain; that it was all for nothing!

He sank even deeper into this unholy, unfamiliar emptiness inside of him, which looked like a massive black hole of which the depth was unknown.

The loud deafening sirens of the nearing emergency vehicles brought him partially back to life, back to the light, and his eyes flew open, watching everything around him unfold like a slow-running movie.

All the voices sounded muffled, like he was under water trying very hard to make out what they were saying.

It felt like a very bad nightmare which he was trying desperately to wake up from, but he couldn't, hard as he tried, he just could not.

He slid down against the wall, brick by brick, until he felt his rubber soles pressing into his muscular flesh, but he didn't really feel it.

All he felt was the black hole he was once again disappearing into. David closed his tired eyes.

They felt so heavy.

In the distance he heard cries.

Was it cries of joy, or cries of despair? He couldn't be sure, but it didn't matter anymore.

He saw a twisted mountain bike floating past, he also saw sparkling emerald eyes before they dissipated from his ailing sight, and then he saw one final glimpse of a blind woman bending before him, her golden cross gleaming in some strange light, but again, he couldn't be sure.

It was completely dark now and absolutely silent.

David slowly let go.

It was time to go home.

CHAPTER 8: COMING HOME!

When he opened his eyes again, after what felt like an eternity, David saw the brightest of bright light.

"Hello David," he heard the crystal clear voice say.

Gradually, his light-brown eyes started to focus again. He began to recognise the very familiar surroundings he was in, although – to his very own astonishment and shock – this sacred place had already faded from his overwhelmed and overburdened consciousness.

"Welcome home," he heard the very familiar voice say. It filled his two ears with hallow sounds.

His light-brown eyes, on the other hand, were being regaled by the most beautiful, serene images. The very first thing he noticed was the exceptional, rare, bright light that touched everything with its golden hue.

Even the myriad of flowers vibrated colourfully in its light. Every single plant, you could say, every single organism looked like it danced glowingly in this magical light.

David could see it reflected in the birds' fluttering

behaviour, even the little buzzing bees seemed 3D to him, like he was seeing and hearing every detail in high definition.

David had forgotten about the sacred magic that this place, his home, held.

The air itself felt different to him. David could feel the softness, the tenderness, or was it love itself he felt all around him; he could feel it, smell it with every restful breath he took.

He suddenly realised that all the agonising feelings he had 'just a minute ago', were gone, completely gone. This was so strange.

One minute they're there, and the next minute they're gone, like they never existed – although he could clearly remember them. It was still there, but it didn't bother him. This puzzled him greatly.

"Welcome home, David," he heard the divine voice for the third time. He could identify the deep, calm voice which still filled his recovering ears with hallow sounds.

He knew the man's voice. It wasn't just any man. In fact, it wasn't even a man.

It was Alpine, his age-old mentor: ALPINE.

Alpine wasn't a mere man; he was what you would call 'immortal'. David knew Alpine since he became conscious. He could remember that the very first thing he noticed about his mentor, was his intense bright light.

They all had translucent bodies radiating a shining light, but Alpine's was immense. It completely bowled him over and even then, he found it difficult to look into his pure form.

His light radiated so brightly because Alpine was revered as one of the wisest saints of all time.

And that was exactly what he was: a SAINT.

They all were, in fact, but Alpine was – besides The Grey One – the purest of them all! They referred to Alaca as 'The Grey One'; he was in charge of everything and everyone. Although a saint would be typically seen as kind and gentle, possessing only love and good in them, Alaca was feared, just a little bit, by the other saints.

Why? Being the wisest scared them a little for he knew and understood absolutely everything. Knowing that, set the bar very high for everyone, even for the great Alpine. They had to hold themselves to that standard at all times.

"David, are you all right?" asked another familiar voice. David loved that specific voice; it belonged to one of his closest brothers. Agtees looked at David with deep concern.

He did not look like the David he knew nor remembered. David, still in his physical form, looked at them with his light-brown eyes. He knew that he would still appear as David for quite some time, because he stayed on earth longer than anticipated.

Agtees helped David up and couldn't help but notice his heavy frame; he even looked bigger than Agtees remembered. He assumed that they would have Ambliss – David's real name – back in no time, but it would seem that he was severely mistaken. He was in worse shape than they all expected.

David couldn't stop staring at his fellow saints. He also couldn't tear away his gaze from his heavenly, paradisian surroundings. David felt overwhelmed all over again, but this time it was in a good way.

He was being overwhelmed by his home - his home; his fellow saints who all dripped with honest to God goodness; and finally his own self which slowly started to stir deep inside him.

His eyes started tearing up while Agtees tried looking over unobtrusively towards Alpine.

Alpine was calmness itself, he did not even bat an eyelid. It was as if he knew what was going on inside of David. He instinctively turned and gave David a hug.

Agtees knew that his hugs were not just a hug, they had the power to smooth over whatever was wrong or felt wrong.

David immediately felt less overwhelmed and more himself. He has forgotten how effective those hugs were and how they made words feel utterly unnecessary.

He has also forgotten about himself; about how much power he really had, especially in this place. It was formidable and to think, they all had it – only God had more power. God's power was the ultimate power and it flowed through ALL of his creation.

This Godly power which was in fact pure love, pure goodness flowed through everything – amazing.

Alpine and Agtees slowly took David into one of their magnificent temples. These temples weren't really sacred. They were rather used for their true purpose which was a place of quiet where each saintly brother could do their work.

Their work, David thought to himself, finally coming to terms with his divine surroundings and his brothers' genuineness.

In the temple stood a few familiar 'faces'. They all had faces, each with their own unique features even though their bodies appeared translucent.

David recognised Aramees, Archean and Addie. They were all in a meditative state. David knew exactly what happened in that state. That was when a saint did his saintly duty of saving people.

What a job he thought with a wry smile. Then he remembered the disconcerting reason for his time on earth...

"Wow, David. Is it really you? I missed you brother." David heard the sweet voice of Addie. Addie was like a child – young and pure – and they always referred to Addie as the baby. Addie didn't mind being called that for he knew that their intentions were good. It was actually a compliment, because maintaining your purity can be challenging at times.

Especially when humans are involved, and they usually are!

That was what every saint did: providing salvation to humans.

They could do that very well, because they all had truth running through their 'veins' and a built in moral compass. They all knew right from wrong and to do good was embedded in their 'DNA', their very core.

The tricky part, however, was to get humans to do the same. They had the tools to do so; they inspired humans to do the right thing.

Because it was the right thing to do, right, David asked in silence. He knew that you could inspire them all you like, but there was this pesky thing called FREE WILL standing between your real inspiration and them doing the right thing.

David remembered full well that most of the time they did not do the right thing or what is good for that matter. They almost always chose the path that would lead to their own selfish gain or towards their own selfish advantage; no matter the consequence...

He learned that one the hard way.

"David, David, can you hear me?" the sweet voice belonging to young Addie asked again, this time with more urgency. David looked at him, at his sweet, innocent 'face'.

"Yes, Addie. I can hear you. I know I've been away for quite some time, but I can still hear and see you. All of you." He slowly looked over each 'face' finally resting his bright, brown eyes on his widely respected mentor, Alpine.

David knew what was coming; he had known for quite some time.

Alpine opened his 'mouth' to say what David knew he was going to say. David steadied himself, because he knew those words would be true and therefore hard to hear. But in this world, there was no hiding from the truth. It was wired into their 'DNA', into their 'brains', in each and every one of them for Christ's sake, David thought, his eyes cast down.

He had no choice, he would have to stare it in the face, whether he wanted to or not, whether he liked to or not!

"David, my brother, I know you had a hard time. I know you had great struggles that wreaked havoc inside of you: they still do. I see that they had raged so fiercely in you that it broke you and then caused you to return home."

David kept his eyes down. He wasn't ready yet. To stare that much prated truth in its eyes would take a lot of courage – courage he did not have at that moment.

At the same time, Archean excused himself followed by Aramees and sweet Addie. Agtees still lingered but after a quick, stern look from Alpine, he also left, waving quietly at David.

David smiled and felt a little tug at his heart. He realised only then how much he missed Agtees. Agtees was always so easy to get along with and he seemed to understand David better than he did himself. It also gave him a small amount of courage and David hoped that it would be enough for what was coming.

"David, are you ready to talk now?" Alpine asked in his ever compassionate and sincere voice.

David finally looked him in the 'eye' and replied that he was. "Good," Alpine answered and the less desired conversation began.

"I feel that I have failed," David opened the ponderous, but much needed, conversation with these considerable words. Alpine looked at him, his loving, pure essence radiating all the while, and then lovingly put his glowing 'arm' around him. He impressed upon David that they should sit on a nearby marble bench. David sat down immediately, relieved for the support beneath him and also for being able to take a load off. It somehow made him feel lighter, or perhaps it was Alpine's presence beginning to take effect on him.

"Why do you say that?" Alpine inquired into David's apparent discontent. David looked at Alpine more easily now. He was unsure of where to begin and how to...

"Why don't you start at the beginning, David?" he asked gently and encouraged him further, "take your time. This is your moment." He gave David a big 'smile' – which was rare although you could always feel his caring nature and his friendly manner – and patiently waited for him to unburden himself.

"I left... I left because I felt that I could do God's work better than Him. I know how that sounds, but that was how I felt at that moment."

He looked down, pondering his following words. Alpine watched David caringly; he knew how difficult all of this was for David. It all boiled down to soul-searching, sheer soul-searching. David was neck-deep in it, but lucky for him, he was nearing the end. He just didn't know it yet, but he will. Very soon, Alpine thought.

"I thought that I could do better. I thought that on Earth at least, I could have a real effect. I would be able to help people even if it meant one by one. But I soon realized that it would take me many, many lifetimes to achieve that."

David shifted his position on the hard surface. The marble wasn't so kind to his physical form. He has forgotten a lot of things, but it was coming back to him slowly but surely.

Alpine kept silent. He knew it was now or never, so he let David explain himself in his own way and in his own time.

"I always thought that God did not care about humans or the planet. All the suffering, the killing amongst each other, how they are destroying the Earth... And nobody seemed to care, not even God. How can he just allow all that suffering and all the destruction to continue?" David took a deep breath; the hardest part was coming.

"I worked harder on saving people. I thought I could do better as I already mentioned. The next step for me was to go there (Earth) and do it myself, do it better! But to my complete disillusionment, it took too long – setting things right – AND as it turned out, I, David, needed Him too."

"*I* needed saving. Especially after... Oh my God! Rick!" he shouted while remembering the accident, the black leather case with the gold letters.

"Rick," he said again, anguish written all over his face.

"How could God let such tragedy take place? How can He just sit there and do nothing?"

His voice climbed a few more octaves and broke. Then David broke down, again. Through teary eyes he asked: "How can God let these things happen... all the suffering... all the hurt... the killing..." Then he stopped.

Alpine rested his glowing 'hand' upon David's shoulder. This calmed him a little bit, just enough to help him see what Alpine was about to show him.

Through thick black clouds he could make out figures. He looked more closely and the image became clearer. Clear enough for him to see that Sarah was bending over a still form lying on a bed. It looked like a hospital bed.

David suddenly sat up straight. Alpine had all of his attention now. The blonde girl, it would seem, was talking to... a man...

It was Rick! David felt over-joyed. He felt immense relief.

Everything was not in vain!

"Do you see David?" asked the familiar voice. "Yes! I see!" He almost didn't get those words out. Rick's eyes were closed, but he was ALIVE!

Rick was alive!

The realization dawned on him again and again. Rick was alive!

"The accident itself, the experience itself was horrible, but necessary. For now the two of them are together. It may not be the ideal circumstance, but they are together. This accident caused them to be on new paths and these two paths are intertwined."

"So you see, David, all is not lost. Here, at least, you have a happy ending."

"And for all the other apparent misery on Earth, you can blame God all you like. But if you look closely you will see and maybe realize that people cause all this misery and destruction, not God."

"You have forgotten that humans have free will and that causes them to do what they want to do. As we know, this is not necessarily always good or right. We always inspire them to do the right thing, to do good, but mostly they don't. You know why."

David finally looked up into Alpine's shiny 'face'. He could see that what he had said is true, oh so true, and this saddened him.

He always thought that people would choose to do the right thing, because it is the right thing to do.

"Don't be hard on them, David. Humans choose what they choose not because it is necessarily right and good, but because it is easy. Doing the right thing is too hard for them. So, these choices usually have negative consequences and coupled with their drive for selfish gain or to have an advantage (for themselves), can have devastating effects – as you have seen," Alpine explained in his usual calm and honest manner.

David had forgotten some truths and shockingly pointed that out to himself. He also realized at long last, thanks to Alpine's superb mentoring, that it was not God who allowed all these bad things to happen, it was the people themselves!

Due to their ambivalent nature they allowed these things to happen and even worse, continue to let it happen.

They do these things to one another, it's not God's

doing!

For the first time in his life, David felt that he finally had all the puzzle pieces, and he could now see clearly. For the very first time, he could see clearly and above all, he understood.

David ultimately had to accept these truths, whether he liked them or not, and with his age-old mentor's help, he did. He accepted these truths and it felt like a heavy burden has been lifted from his heart and from his life.

David smiled. Probably the widest smile in a long time. He finally felt peace – long overdue, but precious peace – claim his heart.

David was home, and he was saved!

All ten brothers were talking excitedly. There was almost not enough room for everyone to speak, but they did with Ambliss in the middle.

Ambliss finally felt and looked like himself again after a good many 'months'. Although time and space did not exist for these saints the way it did for humans.

Ambliss felt so fortunate for being home and for being among his dear brothers, all nine of them: there was Agtees, his closest friend; 'baby-faced' Addie, sweet Addie; Ananis the peaceful one; Aramees, he had a loving presence; Aerie, as the name implied he was very light spirited; then there was Archean, he was a bit of a magical, playful saint; they also had their very own active saint, Argus; Aleutian on the other hand, was a prim and proper, real saint, also a bit stubborn (he did not deviate one millimetre from their code); and lastly, but by no means least, there was Arnica, hmm, Arnica, if ever there were a female saint, it would have been Arnica (no offence).

David – Ambliss sometimes still referred to himself as David – felt deeply happy.

Happy to be alive; happy to be home; happy to be among his treasured brothers and his favourite mentor, Alpine.

All the busy talking was about David's travels on Earth and what he had accomplished. Granted it wasn't nearly enough, but it was a start and a good one at that.

Alaca himself confirmed Ambliss' good work on Earth and it wasn't as David had feared, all in vain. Alaca approved further visits to Earth, not only for Ambliss but for every saint who wished to go!

Ambliss was the very first saint on Earth and also the very first to walk among humans.

It would seem that Ambliss had started something special, hence the lively discussions taking place. Every saint, even the prim and proper Aleutian, wanted a go at it.

David had indeed started something, something GOOD and something RIGHT!

THE END

ABOUT THE AUTHOR

Jorgi initially studied psychology, but ended up writing instead. Thus she has followed her calling despite what the world dictated.

www.ingramcontent.com/pod-product-compliance
Lightning Source LLC
Chambersburg PA
CBHW020622130626
46552CB00003B/1071